YOU'RE ON YOUR OWN, KID

A Love Story

Cora Dalley

Copyright © 2024 Cora Dalley

All rights reserved

The characters and events portrayed in this book are fictitious.

No part of this book may be reproduced, or stored in a retrieval system, or transmitted in any form or by any means, electronic, mechanical, photocopying, recording, or otherwise, without express written permission of the publisher.

Cover design by Cora Dalley with images from Canva

"We fall back into the past, we jump ahead into the future, and in this we lose our entire lives."

— Thich Nhat Hanh

"Beautiful things should belong to beautiful souls."

— Muriel Barbery, The Elegance of the Hedgehog

CHAPTER ONE

I was a stupid little girl when I told George I loved him. Sunburned and fifteen, the straps of my sundress sliding down my shoulders. He had been twenty. He was kind as he turned me down, he was always kind to me. It was the reason I loved him. And afterwards he left me, standing by the pool while the noise of the party continued indoors, turned to stone by the pain of it.

Life is defined as much by the things you avoid as it is by the things you pursue, and my life had been defined by avoiding George, my best friend's brother, for ten years. Then the wedding invitation was posted through the letterbox, and I couldn't avoid him anymore.

Adam comes up behind me while I'm staring at the doormat.

'A summons?' he jokes, looking over my shoulder.

'Something like that.' Before I can pick it up Adam bends like a gymnast and swipes it out of my reach.

'It's nice foiling.' He turns it over and the silver lettering glints in the light from the wide windows of the hallway. 'Actually, this might be just what I need to talk Jay into putting foiled detail on the hardback.'

He hands it to me and walks back into the kitchen where his husband is cutting up fruit for breakfast. When he's gone I walk back through the hall, clutching the invitation to my chest, past their kitchen, up their stairway lined with framed photos of their wedding day, past their bedroom in which their honey-coloured cockapoo is sleeping, up a second, smaller set of stairs to my little rented room.

I'd known this day was coming. Ever since Frannie had posted a picture of herself and Theo together on holiday in Japan the year before, under a canopy of cherry blossoms, a ring sparkling on her finger. I had texted her congratulations and she had called me a few hours later, crying down the phone in a way that was so unlike the woman I knew.

'You'll be a bridesmaid, won't you Hydie?' Frannie had said, her voice thick with sobs, 'We're having the wedding in Spain, at the chapel where my parents were married. I want you there with me.'

I had agreed in the moment and, after hanging up the phone, had gone hot with panic. The joy and excitement I felt for my oldest friend evaporated as I realised I would inevitably have to see George at the wedding, after all this time. From the day that he had left me standing by the pool at Frannie's party I had done everything in my power to avoid him. When Frannie invited me to her house after school, I would make excuses when I knew he was home from university. I feigned sickness when invited to her eighteenth birthday party, booked a holiday that I knew would clash with her graduation, found reasons to avoid all the big celebratory gatherings in her life. And now I was going to miss her wedding.

I sit on my single bed, in the tiny room I rent from Adam and Jay, doing the same mental dance I've done for a decade. I feel the overwhelming desire to be with my dearest friend, to celebrate the things in her life that are important, to spend time with her warm, loving family who've known me since I was a child. And then I feel the pure liquid terror at the prospect of having to see George again after all these years. It's a fear so overwhelming that I've never been able to get past it.

For a long time, I had coordinated a careful dance to maintain my friendship with Frannie while avoiding her brother. When we no longer saw one another every day at school, we visited one another at university, and in the horrible little flats we each rented as graduates. We've been on holidays just the two of us. Our friendship has been a constant in my life. Her strength and warmth have kept me going through difficult times and I don't know what I would do without her. And still, the fear of seeing George again ignites a deep, animal part of my brain that nothing can overpower. I scan the QR code on the back of the invitation - I RSVP no before I can stop myself. I take a shower once I've heard Adam close the door to his home office and Jay's car start up on the drive, and when I've finished drying my hair and dressing I see that I already have two missed calls from Frannie. I take a deep breath and tuck my phone into my jacket pocket, pulling my satchel over my shoulder and heading out to work.

When I get to Meticulous Ink, Graham has already opened the doors. Every other staff member waits until 08:59 to open the shop. Graham flings the glass doors wide as soon as he's set up the till. He greets me with cheer and a cup of coffee as I step inside, and we say good morning and exchange small talk. Graham is in his seventies, retired from his job as a university lecturer, and began working part-time at Meticulous Ink, before taking over when the previous owner retired.

'I do it mostly for the discount,' he'd said to me when I first joined the team, 'I was spending so much of my money here I figured they could let them pay me for it instead?'

Despite being open early there are no customers, so Graham and I pull boxes out of the back room and begin refilling the shelves. There's a shipment of buttery, faux leather journals, and we put the prettiest colours, the deep teal and the soft caramel, into the window display. We unbox a delivery of

Mother's Day and Easter greetings cards, stocking them on the spinning displays in handfuls. I feel a burst of guilt as I lift out a set of "Congratulations!" cards decorated with cherry blossoms, seeing Frannie's engagement photo in my mind's eye. I haven't checked my phone since I left the house.

I leave Graham organising packs of slippery composition notebooks and go to refill the pen holders. I love this bit of the store with its rows and rows of pens, all in neat piles of different colours: jewel tones and cheery pastels, glitter gel pens and thick bright felt tips. There is a separate area behind the till for more expensive pens. They sit behind glass and we sell them occasionally to collectors and people shopping for special gifts. Some of them cost more than my monthly wage. I much prefer this section, I like to watch customers running their hands along the pens, pulling them out and making timid scribbles on the tester paper. I love the satisfying clatter of them all shifting and nestling back together when one of their number is chosen to leave, like they're penguins huddling for warmth.

There are occasional mishaps, little children overcome with the choice who pull them out and fling them on the ground, a woman with a large backpack one day, who turned abruptly to speak to a friend and dislodged the whole unit. But each time they get mixed up I relish picking them up and ordering them all again, reuniting each lost little pen with its family, putting them where they belong.

At around ten the first few customers come in and I spend the morning helping young women looking for journals, mothers finding fuss-free pens for school, and people looking for gifts. I sell several of the new journals just from people walking past the window display.

'It's busy today,' I say to Graham when we finally find a lull in customers just before noon, and take a moment to make coffee and share biscuits from the cupboard, 'early shopping for Mother's Day I assume?'

'And the Easter Holidays,' he replies. 'When that comes round my two boys go into restocking mode, trying to get the grandkids all set up for the next term.'

'It's been nice.' I say, 'Don't get me wrong I like our team very much, but there's only so long you can go with one person to talk to every day.'

Meticulous Ink had been struggling for years, as all paper products were. They had loyal customers, and business boomed during Christmas and the back-to-school season, but a shop with a very specific stock, that offered only beautiful and luxurious things, would always struggle in times when people needed to buy stationery like they bought everything else, quickly and at the cheapest price they could. As much as I would have loved the shop to be full of people making extravagant, expensive purchases, I could sympathise.

'It feels like we had about five minutes between recessions.' Graham says, as though thinking along the same lines. 'When people could afford the luxury of independent shops, and treating themselves. A few years ago we weren't even the only stationers in the area. We had Parson & Parson's a twenty-minute walk away. They were good people. But when money's tight people will make do with cheaper and worse to protect themselves. Eventually they went under and the couple who ran it moved away.'

'But Meticulous Ink survived,' I say, 'so you must have been doing something right.' Graham gives a rueful smile as he takes up his empty mug.

'That we did. We were closer to the station, and the coffee shops.' He sighs to himself. 'I'll take my lunch now. Call me if you need me.'

I feel bad to have brought down the mood of the morning. It had been busy and bright, with the shop full of the smell of early spring air. Meticulous Ink was doing reasonable business, and the figures showed that the shop was in a good position so long as we had a good Christmas this year. But after another quick flurry of customers in the early afternoon, Graham and I spend the rest of the day alone together. I let Graham go early, to the camembert and red wine dinners I know he has with his wife after longer shifts, and take my time cleaning and tidying, getting the shop ready for the next day.

I stop back at the new journals again, running the pads of my fingers over the smooth cover. I consider treating myself to one the colour of peach sorbet, even though I can't really afford it, when I spot a sliver of something better at the back. I reach into the pile and pull gently and find myself holding a journal in a beautiful dreamy lavender. It's the exact shade that Frannie loves, the colour of her wedding invitations, a colour she wears all the time. I take it to the till, plucking the cherry blossom "Congratulations!" card from the stand on my way. Just before closing it down, I scan both through for myself. I tuck the receipt showing my staff discount into the till drawer before carrying it into the safe, and help myself to a broad sheet of the complimentary wrapping paper we offer, tucking everything into one of our gold-stamped paper bags.

I absentmindedly check my phone as I'm locking the doors to the shop, and my heart skips as I see a stream of messages from Frannie, punctuated by more missed calls. I wait until I'm on the bus to open them.

Missed call

Missed call

WHAT

HYDIE

Missed call

Answer your phone!

What do you mean no?

[A screenshot of my RSVP response]

HYDIE I WANT YOU TO BE A BRIDESMAID

I HAD A WHOLE PRESENTATION BOX

Missed call

Hydie please answer my calls :(

I feel nauseous with guilt, but I've already said no. I can't take it back with no explanation. I can't pass it off as a joke, I would never do that. I consider saying it had been an accident, but then I would have to go to the wedding. I hold the phone in my hands for a few moments, then type.

Hi, I'm so sorry I was at work. We're so short-staffed and people are on holiday that week. I just don't think I'm going to be able to make it. I'm so disappointed xxxxxxx

The message takes almost five minutes to write. I agonise over it, trying to categorically rule myself out of attending while causing her as little pain as possible. When I'm back at my flat I make dinner for myself, Adam and Jay. By the time Adam emerges from his home office and Jay comes back through the door with their cockapoo, Millie, I've roasted salmon fillets and plated them with asparagus and green beans, cooked in lemony oil, and garlic rice.

Adam and Jay are a busy, always-on couple, who would live on expensive dinners out and hastily chopped crudités if they didn't have me around, so we made an agreement after my first few weeks of living with them. They keep the fridge stocked with fresh food, and I cook dinner for the three of us whenever I'm in. I'm always in. We talk briefly about our days, Adam's progress designing the new jackets for a series of popular fantasy romance novels, Jay and Millie's day in the office of the publishing house he works for. Adam takes an opportunity to again try to persuade Jay that silver foil belongs on the hardback cover of the latest release they're working on together.

'You see?' He turns the tines of his fork in the light, 'You see how nice that is? Don't you want the book to sparkle like this on the bookshop tables? How could anyone resist?'

'If you're willing to foot the cost of it you can have as much silver foil as you like.' Jay says, unmoved. 'It's all very well you wanting something shiny and lovely, but if we sink money into cover effects and this doesn't sell we've burned a hole in the budget for nothing.'

'Surely the risk makes it exciting?' Adam begins cheekily, but shuts his mouth quickly, when Jay gives him the withering look that he often makes when they're working on the same book. A look that signals that a creative vision has clashed with some figures on a spreadsheet. Adam casts around quickly for something else to say and his eyes land on me.

'What was that lovely card that arrived this morning?' he asks. 'It looked like an invitation. Somewhere nice?'

'It was an invitation to Francesca's wedding.' I say, 'But I can't go.'

Both men look appalled.

'She's your best friend, how can you not go?'

'I'm not free on that date,' I say, 'I have to work.'

'That's what annual leave is for.'

'That's what fake sick days are for.'

I look down at my dinner. It's a pitiful excuse, but I can't tell them the real reason. I've never told anyone.

'I'll see if I can get the time off.' I say quietly.

'It was a beautiful invitation,' Adam muses, 'very Francesca, all that purple. And the foiling, this lovely delicate silver. Of course Jay probably would have wanted it to be matte and boring.' He adds the last sentence quietly.

The couple offer to tidy up but I wave them away. They play badminton with another couple from Jay's office every other week, and I know they hate being late. Once they've left I put on some music for myself. I clear the plates and clean their kitchen, Millie keeping a careful watch from the doorway, ready to rescue any dropped flakes of salmon. Though I only rent a room from Adam and Jay, I often find I have the house to myself. Adam and Jay are out most nights of the week, going to hot yoga and boozy book clubs, and get up at six thirty on sunny Saturday mornings to drive down for a day at the beach with Millie. I usually stay at home and empty their dishwasher.

I should find their bickering over foiled covers and working hours and housework irritating, but I don't. I miss it when they're gone, when there is nobody talking at all.

When I'm done, I feed Millie and go back to my room. I carefully package the journal and write the card, addressing the parcel to Francesca Flores. It won't make things right, I know, but I hope that the gesture will soothe some of the bad feelings. I'd done similar for other events I'd avoided. At Frannie's eighteenth birthday, I brought her present over the next day, and the irritation she'd felt at me melted away as she unwrapped her beautiful new jewellery box, which had cost me almost all the money I had earned from my Saturday job. I had smoothed over my absence from her celebratory drinks after a big promotion by calling the venue ahead of time and putting a bottle of sparkling rosé behind the bar for her.

The next day I take the gift to the post office on my lunchbreak, before sitting on a park bench with my packed sandwiches. Frannie hadn't responded to my message the previous day, and I look at her Instagram, where she occasionally posts cryptic captions when she's upset. There's nothing from the last few days. Her most recent photo is from a week ago. She's sat in an airy restaurant with big windows and white walls, with a glass of white wine in one hand. The other hand is tucking her long black hair behind her ears. Her dark eyes are bright and smiling, the diamond in her engagement ring singing against the light tawny brown of her skin.

CHAPTER TWO

When I finish work on Wednesday evening I see that Jay has messaged me.

We're out at book club this eve. Something arrived for you today, waiting in the living room.

I'm guilty of the occasional impulse order for books or skincare on nights when I'm bored and want to feel something, but I don't remember doing it recently, so I turn the key in the front door without knowing what to expect. I drop my satchel on the ground and scratch Millie's ears as she trots up to greet me.

'Hey gorgeous,' I say, as she wriggles with excitement and pads around me. I hold her happy golden face in my hands for a few moments before she leaps away and bounds back into the living room. I follow her and stop when I see a parcel on the coffee table. I recognise it immediately as the journal I sent to Frannie, unwrapped, rewrapped and repackaged. For one horrified moment, I think she's returned my gift, but then someone speaks.

'Hey gorgeous yourself,' a voice comes from the sofa at the back of the room and I look up to see her in the flesh.

'Frannie!' I call out in delight, hurrying through the living room with my arms out, forgetting why she must have come to see me. She stands and gives me a stiff hug, and we stand in awkward silence for a few moments.

'Do you want a drink?' I say, partly to fill the icy feeling that Frannie, who normally speaks enough for two, is creating.

'A cappuccino out of that fancy coffee machine in the kitchen is the least you can do at the moment.' she says.

I go into the kitchen, hearing her fussing with Millie as I make us both cappuccinos. I dust cinnamon across the foam just as she likes it. When I bring the drinks back through, Frannie's face has softened. With her high cheekbones and strong features she can look intimidating at times, but now she's holding the parcel in her hands and looking at the card with her lips pressed together. I sit down beside her and place the drinks on the coffee table.

'Why did you send this?' she asks.

'It's an engagement present.' I say.

'You already sent an engagement present. You sent flowers and a card when I first got engaged. *This* was a cop-out.' I look at my knees.

'It's been months since I've seen you, and even that was just a quick lunch. You didn't come to my engagement party. You didn't come to the housewarming last year when Theo and I moved. You didn't come to my birthday this year. And now you're not coming to my wedding. Have I done something? Are you angry with me? Because as far as I can see, my best friend is pulling away from me and I have no idea why.'

When she stacks the events up like that I realise how awful it all sounds. I'd met her for coffee and lunches when we were in the same neighbourhood after university, and I had visited her new house a few days after the housewarming with an aloe vera plant. But the more her life accelerates through these important adult stages, the more big moments I miss. And Frannie doesn't know that I agonise over each excuse, trying to negotiate with myself. How can I see my best friend, when I can't bring myself to see her brother? And each time I bail, all Frannie sees is her friend's absence. For a second I consider just telling her, but I can't face it. Hating myself, I pull my most powerful card.

'I don't have a high-flying corporate job like you. I work in a stationery shop. I can't always afford these things you know.'

It's a low blow, and it's only partially true. Though my job doesn't pay well, my rent is low and my outgoings are minimal. I could budget for most of the events I turn down. It works though, Frannie fidgets with the cuff of her blazer.

'I know, I know. I appreciate that. I would never ask you to spend loads of money on me, but if you're worried about the costs for my wedding you don't need to. Everything is being sorted out so guests barely have to pay a thing. Please say you'll come.'

I look into her face. Though she has always looked a little older than her age, right now she looks young, the way she looks when she's concealing hurt feelings. I've seen the expression before, after failed exams and breakups.

'I realise we've lost touch a little bit, but you know your friendship means the world to me. I wanted to come over to ask if there was any way to make it work. If you're busy, maybe we can find a way to fly you out just for the ceremony and back the same day. It's only a few hours flight to Spain. We could do the bridesmaid prep with you on a video call? Then it would only be that one weekend.' She looks pleading.

'I miss you. My whole family misses you. Mum was so upset when you weren't at the housewarming. It's been years, she still thinks you're that scrawny blonde teenager nervously poking at her plate of aloo gobi. I had to find a photo to prove you have in fact turned into an adult at the same time as me.'

She crosses her legs on the couch. 'I did the maths,' she says, 'you know, the last time you saw George was my sixteenth birthday party? Do you even remember that?'

'Do you?' I deflect quickly. 'You had so much Prosecco I thought you were going to be sick.'

Frannie laughs, 'Me? That's not how I remember it. You had half a glass and I found you by the pool twenty minutes later looking like you were about to pass out. My Dad had to take you home, remember?'

I nod, amused that this is her version of events. The details are right, but a crucial element is missing. Frannie takes my silence as a cue to get back on topic.

'Just say you'll try and make it work for me. I want to finally be able to have everyone special to me together in one room, and if I can get both the Spanish and Indian sides of my family to fall in line and get themselves organised, I can't accept you being the one straggler missing from it all.'

I sigh. I can't bear the thought of seeing George again. But I also can't bear to let Frannie down. And as the two feelings tussle in my mind, love edges out fear.

'I'm sure I can make it work. Let me check my schedule.'

Frannie cries out with relief and hugs me. I hold her close, my feelings in a tangle, but when she lets me go we start to chat all about her wedding plans, and when Adam and Jay return with pizzas and a leftover bottle of gin from their book club I forget the panic sitting in my chest, enjoying the time I'm getting to spend with my very best friend.

Fifteen Years Ago

I had met Frannie in primary school, back when everybody called her Francesca. I had been the one to start calling her

Frannie, and it has become the name she uses for herself, even in job applications and serious correspondence. Even her parents call her Frannie now, the name sounding slightly different in each of their accents.

We had been pushed together by the teachers, who hoped our opposing personalities could balance one another out. I was shy, as watery and pale as my blonde hair and light eyes, never speaking in class or raising my hand. I would spend lunch breaks alone, reading books and doing quizzes in magazines in the corner of the playground, as far away from the other children as I could get. Then one day, when we were in our fourth year, our teacher rearranged the classroom seating and put us next to one another.

At first, I was deeply unimpressed. Francesca had always been one of the loudest in the classroom, disruptive and sporty, with sharp features even as a child. At eight years old she had looked like a small adult, one of those children who already wears the face they'll have for the rest of their life. Her appearance and attitude intimidated me, and I had stayed as far away from her as possible. Now we were suddenly being paired for projects and study groups. I wondered if I had done something bad at school, if the teachers were trying to punish me with this loud, irritable girl who answered back in class and would gleefully break a rule, just to see if she could get away with it. I spoke to her only when I absolutely had to, and she in turn would badger me with questions and comments, trying to provoke me into an argument. I wondered more than once if she was deliberately trying to make me cry.

Then, one day, we had finished our classes, and were each pulling our backpacks from our lockers to take home. Francesca went to push past me abruptly as I looped my bag around my arm. We collided and, as we tried to part, something caught, and we were each unable to move. I still remember the moment when I looked down and saw what had happened.

'You like Star Girlz?' Francesca asked, as if daring me to say yes.

'You like Star Girlz.' I whispered back, stunned.

It was a stupid thing to say on both our parts. Everybody liked Star Girlz. The four-part girl band was, at the time, a pop cultural phenomenon, most of our classmates in school liked them, knew the words to their biggest songs and could do the most popular dance routines. But very few of them were devoted enough to be a subscriber to their magazine. I had begged my parents for it, because the subscription came with a collectible charm bracelet. My father had bought the full-year subscription for my birthday present. I realised later that he had spent this extravagant amount of money out of guilt because by the time it came to renew, one year later, he had moved out.

When the first issue arrived, I sat on the doormat and tore open the welcome pack that housed the chunky braided bracelet, then waited for each subsequent issue, which came each time with a little clip-on charm, with a special insert in the magazine explaining its meaning. The first was a moon, which represented their debut single *Meet Me at Midnight.* After that came each of the band member's birth flowers, their favourite animals, an apple to represent their first world tour starting in New York. We weren't allowed to wear jewellery in class, and so I would wear my bracelet in the morning until I got to school, attach it carefully around my bag before putting it in my locker, then clip it back onto my wrist at the end of the day as I stepped out of the gates. The charms built up on the bracelet, and I would curate them as though they were an art installation, choosing an arrangement every day before clipping them in place while my Mother called for me from the front door. The most beloved charm of mine had come on the month of my birthday. A heart-shaped charm in which was set a purple precious stone, an Amethyst, my birthstone. Every subscriber received this charm when their birthday came around, and the charms were in fact glass replicas of the real gems, but it had made me feel as though the Star Girlz had sent something just for me.

It was this bracelet that had caught on Francesca's bag, snagged it by the birthstone charm. It was tangled with something sparkly wrapped around the strap of her backpack and, when I looked closely, I saw it was another birthstone heart, wrapped around an identical bracelet, thickly loaded with collectable charms. Neither of us moved, both held in place by a bracelet we were terrified to break.

'When's your birthday?' she had whispered, looking down at my charms as though affronted by them.

'February,' I replied.

'I wish my birthday was in February,' she said, 'purple's my favourite colour. My birthday is October.'

Her charm was a pale opal, almost transparent. I could see why she wouldn't like it, it almost looked as though there was no charm at all. And yet when I turned my head I saw the rainbows sparkling beneath the surface. It was as though the stone secretly contained every colour in the world, and was just hiding it, keeping its beauty to itself.

'Do you want to swap?' I said, 'I think yours is prettier.'

We stared at each other for a few moments and then, moving very carefully, worked in unison to untangle the two bracelets and set our bags down on the floor. We swapped the charms, carefully adding them to our own stacks.

'Thanks.' Francesca said, 'I didn't know you liked Star Girlz. You never join in with the dances.'

When I opened my mouth to reply a car horn sounded from outside and we both jumped to attention and hurried together out of the school gates. I had stood at the entrance of the school to begin the long wait for one of my parents and watched Frannie run to greet her own father with a hug. A handsome man with the same black hair, he kissed her on the top of the head and she got into the back of a large car. I caught a glimpse of a tall boy in his early teens in the seat beside her, in the uniform of the local middle school.

The next day before classes started Francesca walked up to me with a handful of small plastic sachets that she dropped on the desk.

'I have doubles,' she had said, 'let me know if you want to swap any.' I brought in my duplicates the next day, and we spent our lunchtime carefully sorting through and trading them. It was the quietest Francesca had ever been in a classroom, meticulously lining up the charms in neat rows to work out who was missing what.

The following week Francesca had coaxed me into joining in a choreographed dance routine that needed a fourth dancer. I had done the dance in my room a hundred times, rewound and replayed my cassette tape of the song over and over again until I could do it perfectly, even without the music. Francesca and I had become exasperated with the other girls, a giggly pair who couldn't take it seriously, and the two of us took charge, strong-arming them into listening to us and following our instructions. We brought in our magazines and read them side by side at lunchtime, calmly turning the glossy pages in unison, or practised the dances in the mirrors of the school bathrooms. A teacher came to find us while we were spinning in circles, singing their lyrics at the top of our lungs. We should have been in our seats five minutes before. It was the first time I'd ever been in trouble, and I followed Francesca and the teacher back to our class and took my seat beside her, both of us flushed and giggling.

CHAPTER THREE

Before I can come to terms with what I've agreed to, Frannie is sending me daily emails with links and schedules. I'm suddenly expected to have an opinion on cake flavours, and what shade of caramel suit Theo would look best wearing. The venue at least is a no-brainer, Frannie's family is Spanish on her Father's side, and her grandparents live in a beautiful apartment in Mijas Pueblo, a small town in the municipality of Mijas, pronounced 'Mee-has', set into the heights of the Andalusian mountains, looking out over the Mediterranean Sea. A family friend runs a hotel a short drive outside the town.

'That's why our guests won't have to pay too much.' Frannie had explained, 'Theo and I have our own savings and both sets of parents are contributing. I'm wearing my Abuela's wedding dress so we're only paying to have it altered a little. The wedding itself will be in a little local chapel, and the reception is in a local hotel where the guests can stay. I've spoken to my parents and you'll be staying with me at my grandparents' house, so there'll be no charge at all for you.'

The fact that I don't have to pay is both a relief and a source of anxiety. It removes the best excuse I have. I am officially going to the wedding. I will have to see George again. When Frannie left the house after visiting I had gone up to bed and allowed myself to imagine a few scenarios in which I was still able to avoid it. I considered falling ill at the last minute, or having a family emergency just as I was setting off to the airport. But I feel stupid even thinking about it. I start to irritate myself. That I would seriously consider missing my best friend's wedding out of embarrassment is ridiculous. It occurred to me after Frannie had left Adam and Jay's house, that George may not even remember what I had said to him. It had been ten years ago, and I hadn't seen him since. I had made sure of it. More than that, he might not remember me at all. It is likely that Frannie has brought me up in conversation intermittently, but if he hasn't seen me in a decade, I've probably faded from his mind. Perhaps if he has completely forgotten me, we have the chance to meet again, this time as two adults, rather than a lovestruck teenager and a bewildered twenty-year-old. We could become friends, and I could finally stop worrying about what might happen when I see him again.

I lie in bed taking heart from this thought and, when I reply to Frannie's latest deluge of links the next morning, I feel a flutter of genuine excitement for the first time since the invitation arrived on my doorstep. Full of warm feelings, when Frannie asks me for a song to put on the playlist for the reception, I suggest *Meet Me at Midnight,* the Star Girlz hit from our childhood, that we had danced to together so many times.

That takes me back! she replies as we message back and forth. *I wonder if I still remember the routine...*

If you do, you have to do it on the dance floor in your wedding dress!

Only if you do it with me!

Though Frannie and I had never truly fallen out of one another's lives, it feels good to suddenly be speaking regularly again. We had spent a few years only catching up about big things, and the fresh wedding discussions lead us back to our old talking points; her family's habits, songs and books we're enjoying, and what our old school friends are doing now. Just a few weeks later Frannie invites me to Mijas.

'We need to see the priest, and have some discussions about the venue,' she says, as we sit in narrow wicker chairs outside a small coffee shop with a takeaway cup each. 'But it'll also be nice to have a little break up there together with my family. It's so peaceful. The town is beautiful, this little village in the mountains. We've got a flight to get there in the afternoon, but there's a later flight closer to you, so you may as well take that and we'll collect you at the airport once we've picked up the car. We'll be there before dinner.'

'How much are the tickets?' I say, but Frannie interrupts me before I've finished.

'You're not paying anything!'

'Are you sure?'

'Of course! It's all budgeted for. It's part of the wedding preparations. It's going to be so much fun. Nisha hasn't seen you for ages either! She asked if you still had the pink ombre hair from your graduation photos.'

Nisha is Frannie's sister, and the eldest child of the family, two years older than George. I had known of her before she had known me, an effortlessly cool and unflappable teenager who was always winning certificates and prizes for spelling competitions and chess club, and she had stayed that way as long as I had known her. Sharp and collected, but a little cold, without the fierceness of her younger sister, or the warm glow of her brother.

'Is the rest of your family coming too?'

'Everyone but George.' she says, 'He's staying behind because his *girlfriend* is having some big work event.'

If I didn't know Frannie as well as I do, that sentence would have sounded completely innocuous, but there's a slight exaggeration in the way she says girlfriend that my brain picks up, even if my ears don't quite register it.

'I didn't even know he had a girlfriend,' I say, as neutrally as I can, 'that's how long I've been away.'

'Oh yes, it's not been that long but she's coming to the wedding as his plus one. He's even paying for her flights and their hotel room when we told him he doesn't need to.' She scoffs, unimpressed.

'What a terrible person,' I joke.

'He's just too nice for his own good,' Frannie says.

'That's how I remember him too.' I say. I work hard, perhaps a little too hard, to keep my voice level and expressionless, because Frannie looks at me. I take a sip of my coffee to give myself something to do, and think of something to distract her.

'How is Theo feeling about it all?' I ask, inspiration hitting. 'He's never been out there has he?'

'It will be overwhelming for him, it always is. But it's a good chance for him to get to know that side of the family. He came to Jaipur to meet Mum's parents last year, but he's never met my grandparents on Dad's side'

'Have you met his?'

'I have, they took us to Osaka where they grew up last year, and they met us in Japan after we got engaged. They're lovely, but much calmer and quieter than I'm used to. I'm a bit worried my family are going to scare them. My plan is for them to meet Nisha and George in the next few months, so they get used to the most normal people, and then I'll slowly ease the rest of them in.'

I take off the needed days from the stationery shop from my untouched annual leave, and soon I'm packing the most weather-appropriate clothes I have and trying to choose which book to read on the plane: a chunky thriller novel or an elegant philosophical novel, translated from French. I decide that this is a good chance to meet the rest of Frannie's family before seeing George again, but that when I do, he will barely remember me. I decide that this is a fresh start for us both and that the wedding, instead of a terrifying ordeal, is a chance to shake off the ghosts of that one single event that I have allowed to steal precious moments of my life. I pack both books. I lie in bed the night before the flight, trying not to feel the nerves unspooling in my chest, to feel only excitement. I have barely closed my eyes before my alarm goes and I must leave for the airport in the grey morning.

I leave a cold, gloomy London spitting with rain, and when I step out at the other end of my journey it's as if I've flown to a different universe. The weather is glorious, an expanse of blue sky that makes me feel small and humble, and the warm gentle wind cups my face like a childhood sweetheart. As I leave the glass doors at the front of the airport I see Frannie in a sand-coloured dress and wide sunhat, standing with an obnoxiously large piece of paper on which she has scrawled "HYDRANGEA".

'I'm not responding to that,' I say, feigning walking past her.

'Oh come on, I had this massive sign, "Hydie" would have been too short.'

'Can I see this?' I say, reaching for the sign. Frannie hands it to me and, before she can stop me, I crumple the sign and stuff it into a nearby bin.

'No fun,' Frannie laughs, 'come on, Nisha's got the car parked up here.'

We reach a dusty silver hire car, and Frannie takes my bags and puts them in the trunk.

'Hi, Hydie. How've you been?' Nisha smiles at me from the driver's seat as I get into the back with Frannie.

'I'm okay,' I say back. 'How are you? Long time no see.'

Bizarrely, she looks almost unchanged. Her brows are

stronger and the hair that used to live in a long sleek ponytail has been cut to just above her shoulders, but like Frannie, she is instantly recognisable as the same person I knew ten years ago.

'Hello,' another voice says from the front passenger seat, and a small tanned face looks round at me. It's a little girl, with round eyes, long, light-brown hair and an earnest, heart-shaped face.

'This is Lila,' Nisha says, 'my daughter.'

Frannie often talked about her niece so I wasn't surprised to meet this new-to-me addition to the Flores family.

'Hello,' I wave.

'You're Hydie,' she says, 'Auntie Frannie's friend.'

'I am. Nice to meet you.'

'Lila's going to be my flower girl,' Frannie says, 'do you want to tell Hydie about the dress we've just picked for you Lila?'

We continue on in the pleasant but slightly stilted conversation one has with an eight-year-old as Nisha starts the car. After a long drive through a flat, dry landscape we begin to ascend through the mountains and I glimpse stretches of a clear, bright sea between the trees that line our route.

As we wind around the roads, the town of Mijas Pueblo comes into view, nestled into the mountains like a sleeping cat. I see clusters of creamy white buildings and terracotta-coloured roofs arranged in haphazard streets, occasional pools and patches of green grass are studded through the town, like gems set into plaster. Nisha parks at the hotel which sits a few miles from the town like a huge glittering beetle with its glass windows reflecting the sunlight. From there we walk along a long path up the mountain, wheeling our cases and carrying our bags, until we reach the town. We walk through narrow cobbled streets lined with gleaming white houses until, partway up the incline of the town, we reach a street where Lila points at one of the buildings. She runs ahead and I watch the flash of pink as the soles of her trainers smack against the dusty driveway.

'You didn't bring much.' Frannie says, taking the bag from me and swinging it over her shoulder. I don't reply, but follow her silently towards her Grandparent's house which is similar to most of the buildings in Mijas, with the same wide white walls and orange tiled roof. It makes me think of a large, glamorous woman in a white sundress and straw hat. I imagine Mijas Pueblo as a summer party full of these giantesses, all dressed to impress, who've accidentally arrived in the same outfit and are deciding to make the best of it. Along the length of the building is a balcony, guarded with a railing of thin black iron, and leaning against it are a tall older man with dark curls, and a younger, shorter man in a polo shirt with straight black hair, who I recognise as Theo. The younger man grins as he sees his fiancée walking up the driveway, and Frannie's father waves as we approach. The men turn to go down the stairs in the house to greet us.

The area by the front door is scattered with flowerpots, all painted in glossy jewel-coloured tones, teal and amber and scarlet. Closer to the house I see a small grey cat slinking between the pots and, just a few metres behind it, Lila trying to edge her way towards it, her eyes wide and her lips pressed together in concentration.

'Lila!' Nisha shouts sharply. The cat bolts, disappearing over the garden wall. 'What have I told you about chasing her?'

Lila stands and stamps her foot, crossing her arms petulantly.

'I nearly had her. Why did you do that?'

'Because that cat doesn't want you bothering her. That's why she runs away.'

The girl looks longingly at the spot at the top of the wall where the cat's tail has whipped out of sight. 'But she's so cute. I just want to stroke her head.'

Nisha shakes her head and carries on walking.

'That poor cat. It lives with the family across the road. It was having a fuss-free life before we all showed up, and any time Lila's here it doesn't get a second to itself.'

The noise of talking and activity spills out through the door before we can step inside. The front room, though reasonably large, is rendered cramped by the sheer volume of people inside it. At least fifteen men and women of all ages sitting on sofas, on chairs clearly taken from other areas of the house and placed wherever there is room. A few people standing on the patio in the back having flung open the doors to make more space. A loud cry of delight comes from a tiny elderly lady who sets eyes on Frannie and begins to get up from her chair. Frannie calls to her in Spanish and runs over, saving her from getting up by enveloping her in a big hug. The family descends on us, fawning over Lila, taking Frannie's hand and holding up the ring, embracing Nisha and speaking to me in different levels of English all at the same time, so that I cannot hear the words I understand over those that I don't.

Through the sea of people steps a beautiful, curvy Indian woman in a green dress, with long black hair that, since I last saw her, has become threaded with grey. Frannie's mother beams at me and opens her arms wide. The clinking sound of her bracelets is like the smell of a house I once lived in, the memories flooding back. I gladly step forward and embrace her as her arms fold around me.

'It has been too long my darling,' she says, and I have the surprising feeling that I'm going to cry. Sameera calls her younger daughter over from the group and holds each of our hands.

'How lovely to see you two together again,' she says, 'Frannie please take Hydie upstairs, her room is on the left next to yours.'

'Next to mine? I thought we were giving Hydie the front bedroom?'

'We were, but that room has a desk and George needs it to work from.'

I feel like I am being thrown forward, as though the world has stopped spinning suddenly beneath my feet.

'George is here?' I say, trying to keep my voice level. Sameera smiles.

'Of course, you two won't have seen one another in years! Yes, wonderfully his plans were cancelled. He didn't have time to take leave from work so he's up there on calls. But he'll be down for dinner. Speaking of which,' Sameera looks over her shoulder at where Lila is holding the hems of her dress and spinning while her family adores her, 'you'll both be needed to help with dinner. Feel free to take a few minutes for yourselves but be back down for seven.'

Frannie leads me back to where we brought our things.

'Nisha and Lila are staying at my aunt and uncle's a little way away,' she says, 'so we'll leave their luggage here.'

We take our bags and walk up narrow steps to the second floor, with a long carpeted landing and several doors.

'You're here next to me,' Frannie pushes a door open, white with small blue flowers painted on it, 'shall I knock for you in five minutes? It's always chaos making food but hopefully we can just find a corner and chop things.'

I step into my room, hearing her knock gently on a door further down the hallway and say a casual hello. A muffled male voice calls out in reply. All of a sudden the panic returns. I had come to terms with seeing George eventually, but, all of a sudden, eventually has become today, with no time to prepare.

In spite of myself, I take a look in the small mirror sitting on the windowsill, looking at my skin, dehydrated from the flight and my hair, somehow both unkept and flat. I pull a hairbrush and some moisturiser from my bag and try to wrangle myself back into a presentable person before starting to organise my things. The room is snug but comfortable, with the same faded pistachio-green carpet and dark, wooden furniture as the rest of the house. I unpack my clothes on the small double bed, laying my things out on the crisp white bedding with old-fashioned detailing, before finding them a place in the narrow wardrobe and slightly sticking chest of drawers. I set out my one bottle of perfume, tinted lip balm and books on the bedside table. I take off my clothes and put on a pretty blue sundress, before changing my mind and putting my jeans back on, pulling on a clean white blouse, and meeting Frannie back at the top of the stairs.

CHAPTER FOUR

As we enter the small kitchen at the back of the house, we see that the women have already set to work like a finely tuned ecosystem. Bottles of balsamic vinegar and olive oil are placed on the table, breads are sliced, and cutlery, plates and napkins are retrieved from their drawers and cupboards and carried out to a long wooden table. I stand watching, feeling useless, until Frannie's grandmother holds a nut brown hand out to me and leads me to a long counter, in which fruit and vegetables are piled in wire baskets. She says a sentence in Spanish that I don't fully understand, though I recognise *tomates.* She hands me the knife and sets down a bowl of just-washed tomatoes, fat and brilliant red, still on clipped stems of the vine.

'Big wedges.' Frannie says to me, coming to stand beside me with a basket of small green padron peppers which she rinses under the tap.

'Sorry?'

'Cut them into big wedges, like they're orange slices,' she calls out over her shoulder, 'where are the men? I notice they're not offering to help.' The older women roll their eyes. 'Not in my household,' Frannie mutters under her breath, 'George is on a work call and Theo is upstairs sweeping the balcony for my grandparents. All the other men are sat in the garden.'

I set to work cutting the tomatoes, placing the wedges into a blue ceramic bowl that Frannie's mother places next to me, as she walks past carrying wine glasses.

'Can I help with anything?' A man's voice calls from the hallway, I jump before recognising Theo leaning through the kitchen door.

'Look at you!' Frannie calls to him, 'making my choice in a husband look more and more sensible every day.' One of her aunts tries to shoo Theo away but Frankie steps in with a tea towel.

'The glasses and water pitcher need drying,' she says, taking him to the draining board. 'then put the ice and lemon I just sliced into the pitcher, fill it with water and set everything out.' She kisses him on the cheek and sends him away.

'Your husband is hardworking and you're making him do chores.' another auntie says, shaking her head.

'We're both hardworking,' Frannie says, 'we both work full-time jobs, and we both look after the home.'

I'm so focused on my task, watching the knife slice through the juicy flesh of each tomato, listening to the chatter of the other women, that I don't notice someone else has slipped into the room from the door into the garden, until slim tanned fingers come into my eye line and pick up a wedge of the tomato I've just chopped. I follow the hand as it lifts the wedge up to a full, smiling mouth and takes a bite. It's George. George in a powder blue shirt that contrasts with the warmth of his tanned skin and his dark brown eyes. He winks at me, bites into the tomato and puts a finger to his lips, his other hand holding a phone to his ear, before walking quietly back out of the kitchen before anybody else has noticed him.

I almost laugh. I had spent so long thinking about the first moment we would see each other again, what I would say, what sort of impression I would give, and in the end it had been so quick that I hadn't said or done anything, just stared blankly into his face until he left again. I'd twisted myself into knots worrying about that moment, and then it had come and gone before I could even think.

'Are you alright?' Frannie asks, returning to where she had been standing, and following my gaze through the open doorway.

'Your brother took some tomato,' I say, stupidly.

'Nice of him to show up to be honest,' Frannie says. 'If he's not on the phone with work he's on the phone to his *girlfriend*.'

'Frannie be nice.' her mother says in a warning way, though Nisha makes a face over her shoulder.

'Sorry Maa.' Frannie says, then, when her mother turns her back, exchanges a look with her sister.

Once I've chopped the tomatoes, I'm given fruit to wash and prepare, then I help to carry dishes and wine to the long table in the dining room, which has been laid with a long white tablecloth and sunny yellow napkins. Frannie's grandmother shouts across the garden with surprising force and the cluster of men sitting in the late sunshine lift themselves from their chairs. From another room, Theo and George emerge together and seat themselves at the nearest end of the table. Frannie joins them, and I begin to follow, trying not to worry that I'll go from surviving the first introduction to George to suddenly being trapped in a full evening of conversation with him. But as Frannie beckons to me, while George is pouring water in the tumblers, a soft bronze arm wraps around mine.

'Ah, ah, ah,' Frannie's mother says, 'she's had you long enough, I haven't had a moment to catch up with you.'

I allow myself to be taken away to the other end of the table where Frannie's father Roberto is helping his mother take her seat. He gives a cry of delight when he sees me and embraces me warmly, kissing me on the cheek. He pulls a chair out for me and pours me wine and water before seating himself next to his wife, across from me.

'Now this is a face we've missed,' Sameera says, placing a hand on her husband's arm and looking at me fondly, 'you must tell us all the wonderful things that have kept you so busy. Frannie tells me you work at a beautiful stationery shop?'

It's been so long and yet it's as though I've never been away. The two of them look at me so fondly as I rattle off the small, quiet features of my life. I'm reminded of the times in my childhood they had sat and asked about the books I had been reading, or the music Frannie and I had been listening to. They always listened to us as though we were adults, as though our opinions mattered in a way no other adult had ever done for me. I had forgotten the way their warmth and attention emboldened me to become louder, more forthright in their company. It wasn't until I had grown up that I realised that this style of parenting had produced Frannie and her siblings, all supremely confident in themselves, completely convinced that the things they had to say mattered.

'We are so happy to see you,' Roberto says, spooning potatoes in a thick tomato sauce onto my plate. 'we know you're busy and you have your own life but we were worried you wouldn't be able to be part of this. Frannie would have been heartbroken.'

'I'm sorry I've been away,' I say, 'I've missed you both. I just. I suppose life kept getting in the way...' I trail into silence, trying to think of some way to explain myself.

'You'll never believe what I found the other day,' Sameera says, covering my awkward pause, 'Frannie's little charm bracelet. From those magazines you both used to read, about that band you loved. Do you remember them? I couldn't believe it. I was looking through a box of her old school things in a wardrobe and there it was. There must have been a year when she didn't take it off outside of school. And you were the same, weren't you? Obsessed, both of you.'

'I'm not sure what I did with mine,' I say, trying to remember. 'You're right we must have worn it every minute of every day for years, then suddenly I took it off one day and never put it back on again. I don't even remember doing it. It must be at one of my parent's houses. It might even have been lost when we all moved out.'

'And how is your family?' Roberto asked, a little curtly.

'I think they're okay,' I say, 'I don't see too much of either of them, but they both seem to be happy now, which is good.' It's a sad little answer, and both Sameera and Roberto look at me with a hint of pity. I change the subject quickly.

'How are you both finding being grandparents? Lila seems so sweet, she chatted to us the whole drive here.'

They both light up like a sunrise and launch into a full and comprehensive list of every one of Lila's best qualities, all her achievements, how ahead of the other students she is in every class. How proud they are of Nisha as a mother. I'm happy to stay quiet and listen, their affection for their granddaughter radiates out in warm glowing waves, and I bask in it, lifted by how much people can love one another.

After dinner I help tidy things away. Frannie calls to me and I approach, steeling myself to talk to George, but as I reach them his phone begins lighting up on the table.

'Really?' Frannie says, scowling at him.

George sighs, shrugs, and picks up the phone, pressing it to his ear and walking out of the room.

'I can't believe him.' she shakes her head and I see her tense with irritation and Theo reaches out and gently takes hold of her hand.

'Best to leave him be,' he says, 'he's got enough on his plate without us getting at him.' Frannie's shoulders visibly relax. She nods and turns to me.

'Shall we each take a glass of wine and sit on the balcony?' she asks, 'they're all happy to tidy up, I'm going to take a feminist stance and skive off.'

We take a leftover bottle from the table and find a corner of the balcony upstairs with a good view, the last light of the evening tumbles down the mountainside, into the glittering barrier of the seaside towns that have lit up for the night.

'We'll take you to eat down there one day,' Theo says to me, as he pulls three wicker chairs into position, while I hold the glasses and Frannie pours. 'you'll have the best seafood you've ever tasted sitting at that beach.'

'And the cheapest sangria.' Frannie chuckles.

The night is warm and we drink the soft, juicy red wine and discuss the wedding preparations while some of the inhabitants of the house say their goodnights below us. Pockets of quiet conversation and a radio somewhere near the kitchen form a low, hazy sound that could put me to sleep if I closed my eyes. Movement from just beneath the balcony catches my attention and I look down to see the little grey cat that Lila had chased that morning. She slinks, as though made of water, along the edge of the low stone wall, avoiding the stripe of light made by the just-open door to the house, her eyes turned to two silver coins as they reflect in the dark.

As I watch, the strip of light begins to widen and I realise someone is carefully opening the front door. A small shadow begins to emerge and, from beneath the balcony, Lila creeps onto the front drive, trying to approach the cat. I watch her as she takes slow, cautious steps along the paving, making each movement as silent as she can. I can feel her desperation to reach the cat, to have the opportunity to prove herself to it. But before she can reach her Nisha shouts sharply from the sitting room.

'You'd better not be after that cat, Lila!'

Lila stops in her tracks. The cat, looking round and seeing her, scarpers away. Lila stands for a while looking out at where the cat had been, holding her thin arms around herself. I look away, not wanting her to know I have seen her failure.

'Poor kid,' Frannie whispers, 'Nisha means well, but she doesn't need to police everything she does. She's not a bad kid for wanting to pet a cat for God's sake.'

'She thinks she's bothering it.' I say.

'Of course she is. That's what kids do, they make a nuisance of themselves. I love Nisha, she's a great mum in so many ways, but it's like she wants Lila to be completely quiet and still when she's not doing something Nisha wants. Like she's a little doll you can turn off.'

I don't reply, and neither does Theo. We both understand that Frannie's opinion of Nisha is something she is allowed to express, and that neither of us are welcome to add to it. I look back over at where Lila is standing, and see that she's watching something in the distance.

A boy is walking up the driveway, perhaps eleven years old, in scruffy shorts and flip flops, holding something in his arms, and when he steps further into the light I see that it's the cat, nestled contentedly against his chest.

'Who's that?' I ask Frannie, who cranes shamelessly over the balcony to get a good look at him.

'It's the neighbour's son,' she says in a hushed voice, 'I think his name is Camilo. We don't see much of him, I think he lives with his other parent somewhere else in Spain most of the time. He must be visiting.'

As we watch, the boy walks up the drive to where Lila is standing. After casting a wary glance back at the house, she takes a few steps to meet him. They exchange a few hushed words, and Lila shakes her head. It occurs to me that Lila cannot speak much Spanish yet, and that the young boy probably doesn't speak much English. Undeterred by the language barrier, The boy leans forward, holding the cat towards Lila. The soft grey head emerges and sniffs the air cautiously. Lila reaches her fingertips towards it, gently brushing between its ears. The cat leans into her touch, and Lila's posture relaxes as she strokes the cat more confidently, down its back and under its chin. With a huge grin on her face she looks up at the boy, who smiles back down at her.

He's taller, though only by a head, with a mop of hair that is darker than hers, chestnut curls catching the light. They gaze at one another longer than is comfortable, and I want to scrape my chair, or drop something, to break whatever little enchantment is weaving between them. But I'm spared by Nisha's voice calling again from inside the house. The two of them part, Lila skipping back into the house, and the young boy carrying the cat back away through the gates and across the road.

'Well look at that,' Theo says, 'you go chasing a cat and find yourself a little boyfriend.'

'Don't say anything,' Frannie says, 'Nisha will only flip her lid. We'll keep an eye on her.'

When the last of the light has faded and the sky has turned deep indigo we tuck our chairs away and Frannie shows me back to the landing where my bedroom is. I cross the thin carpet to the door with the flowers painted on, wash my face and change, and am asleep before I can even wonder what the time is.

CHAPTER FIVE

I wake with my heart gently thudding against my chest. It is just past seven in the morning and the house is silent. I consider pulling the duvet across myself and trying to sleep again, but the lure of the empty morning is too tempting after a night full of voices.

I dress quietly, pulling on a powder blue sundress that sweeps to my shins. I apply sunscreen carefully, noting patches of skin that I missed the day before, thin crescents around my wrists and elbows that have caught the sun and turned pink. I put the suncream in my small tote bag with the French novel I had packed, and my water bottle. I braid my hair in a band around my head and leave the bedroom as quietly as I can.

At the end of the hallway, one of the bedrooms is open, the bed already made, but when I go downstairs there is nobody around. I fill up my water bottle at the kitchen tap and decide to take a walk into the town that I had only glimpsed the day before. I push the door open and walk up the drive, past the little grey cat stretching out on the low wall in the sunshine. The walk takes me down a series of narrow stone steps and cobbled streets past stretches of white stone apartments. A few elderly people sit on wicker chairs by their front door, drinking coffee and smoking cigarettes.

The town centre is beautiful in the quiet, cool morning, a circle of paving stones in dove grey, cocoa and eggshell in a geometric pattern, studded with tropical trees and surrounded by cafes, restaurants and shops. Shop staff prepare to open their doors through the windows as I walk past, and a few cafes already have their tables and chairs set outside. I approach the nearest one, thinking of reading my book with a coffee under the ivory-pink awning. Each little round table is laid with a gingham cloth, blue garden chairs set at each side. I walk between them and step into the coffee shop. A few of the tables are already occupied with people reading newspapers or battered paperbacks in silence.

I approach the counter to order a drink, looking around the blue-painted walls for a good seat, and my breath catches in my throat. Sitting alone at a table, laid out with papers and a laptop, is George. He hasn't noticed me, his gaze instead fixed intently on his screen, the fingers of one hand to his temple. I realise I haven't looked at him properly yet, only glancing at him in the kitchen, down the stretch of table at dinner the night before, and I find my eyes lingering on him, picking out the differences between the man in front of me, and the boy I had been so besotted with.

He looks up as I'm staring, straight into my face. I look back at him blankly for what feels like an age, though half a second later he breaks into a smile and waves me over. I approach numbly, putting on what I hope is a casual, friendly expression.

'Hello trouble,' he says, gesturing to the chair opposite him.

'I don't want to disturb you.' I look at the papers in front of him.

'No, please, you're a welcome break from this.' he stands and walks around the table and I feel my skin heat as I wonder if he's going to hug me, but instead he pulls a slim brown wallet from his pocket.

'I need another coffee. Can I get you something?'

I squint at the board, which has images instead of words, the outlines of coffee cups filled in with stripes of white, brown and clear to represent the variations of coffee, water and milk that go into a latte, a cappuccino, a flat white.

'What's the pink one?' I ask.

'A good question. I'm wondering about the green one,' he smiles down at me. 'How about we order both and find out? I'll take the green if you try the pink.'

'That feels like it could be dangerous.'

'The true danger is not taking the chance, surely?'

I laugh. 'Fine, but if they're disgusting, you'll need to drink them both.'

'Deal.'

I take the spare seat and try not to fidget while he orders at the counter. He's wearing pale, stone-coloured trousers and a loose, cream short-sleeved button-down with a wide collar. It makes the deep colour of his skin more bronzed in contrast. As he turns round I look quickly ahead of myself as though staring into space, then, as though his movement has caught my eye, look back and smile casually as he approaches.

'Look at these.' He sets the two drinks down on the table, both in glass-walled mugs. The one he takes is a fresh, grassy green and smells botanical. The one he leaves for me is a dreamy soft pink, with clouds of frothed milk across the top. 'Predictably mine is matcha. Yours is something with rose in it. Give it a try.'

He walks back to the counter as I cautiously poke at it for a few moments with my teaspoon, watching the steam rise, and returns with two puffy croissants that smell incredible.

'Good idea,' I say, 'just in case we need something to take the taste out of our mouths.'

'If you hate it I'll buy you something else,' he says, 'now, if you'll forgive me for starting with a cliché, it's been too long. How have you been?'

'I know. I'm sorry, life kept getting in the way.' It was the line

I'd used on his parents the night before. 'But I'm doing okay.' I say a few sentences about the stationery shop and my living situation. He smiles and nods, as though I'm saying something interesting. I had forgotten how dark his eyes were. Darker than those of his sisters, which are each brown, but shot through with flashes of tawny or pewter. His are a flawless perfect mahogany, I can see myself in them as I talk.

'That all sounds amazing,' he says, 'I bet you're perfect at a stationery shop, I can just see you helping little kids pick out gel pens, and helping someone get that perfect journal as a gift for a friend.' I smile like a child and look bashfully into my lap.

'And what are you doing now?' I ask, and am surprised when George gives a huge weary sigh and puffs his cheeks out.

'I'm doing exactly what I've always wanted to do. A proofreader for high-flying corporations.'

'Oh,' I remember that that is indeed exactly what he always wanted to do. When I last saw him ten years ago, he had been interning at technical writing agencies while on summer break before returning for his third year at university, using his sharp eye for detail and memory for the strange quirks of grammar in a way that could actually make some money. 'You sound thrilled about it.'

'I shouldn't complain. The money is so much better than I would have proofreading in other industries, but at the same time it's not exactly inspiring. I feel like I spend all my life looking at things people have worked really hard on and thought a lot about, and picking out their mistakes.'

'I don't know if you need to look at it like that,' I say, 'if you were looking through something I'd written I would feel like you were just helping me realise the best version of what I'm trying to create. Like you're adding knowledge I don't have to make it stronger.'

He tilts his head, fidgets with a slim silver band on his thumb.

'That's a nice way to look at it. I should come to you every time I feel bad about something, and ask you to find the positives. It doesn't stop the fact that I need to get all this done in the next couple of hours. That's why I got up so early to come out here. We're an hour ahead. The London office hasn't started up yet so I won't be fielding calls for a few hours.'

'Shall I let you get on with it?' I ask, 'I can take my drink away and entertain myself.' I reach into my bag and pull out my book. He smiles again.

'If you don't mind me typing and shuffling paper around, I would love it if you stayed here with me while you read. I think I'd just like the company.'

'Sure. But first, we should try our drinks so we know if we need to get up and order something else.'

'Sounds good. Let's do this together.'

We clink our mugs together, both laughing a little at the silliness of it, before taking a sip. Mine is a cappuccino, but spiced and floral, the light, beautiful flavours of rose and cardamom singing through the deep coffee and foamy milk.

'It's lovely,' I say, 'I would order this again. How's yours?'

He puts the cup down as he swallows, licks his lips as he thinks.

'You know that lovely smell of freshly cut grass?'

'I do.'

'It's not quite as nice when it's a taste.'

I laugh. 'Oh no, do you need another drink?'

'No, I'll keep going. It might grow on me. It's not bad. It's just sending some very strange signals to my brain.'

'If you're sure.'

We settle into a companionable silence. I open my book,

privately pleased I'd bought the sophisticated French novel rather than the thriller I'd started on the plane. It is a beautiful book about a woman, a young girl and a quiet Japanese man who bond as outsiders living in a luxurious Parisian apartment building. It had captivated me when I had started it, but now I can't settle to reading when I open it in my lap. Instead I sneak tiny glances at George as he works, reading the words on the page as if they haven't been translated, using them like stepping stones, my eyes jumping across a few lines until I feel I can chance another look up.

It's strange that he's so close, across from me as though we had met regularly for coffee over the last decade. As though this was part of some comfortable routine we had in some other reality where we hadn't faded from one another's lives. I wonder if this was how it could have been had I never spoken to him that night. Perhaps if Frannie and I hadn't snuck out with a bottle of Prosecco and sat on the steps, if that hadn't made me brave and stupid, drawn to where he had been standing by the hazy blue light of the water. I think about the boy who had been standing there. Though he had always been beautiful to me, at twenty his hair had been much shorter, cut to hide the curls as best he could. and he had been less broad, thinner in the chest and shoulders. Ten years later he has grown into himself, his tall frame filled out broad and strong, his jaw heavier, strong enough to carry the large dark eyes and full mouth. His hair is still short, but his dark curls have grown enough to frame his face and, as I glance at him, I notice a couple of threads of grey around his temples and forehead, turned gold as they catch the light like the crest of a wave.

Eleven Years Ago

Frannie had chosen the venue because of the swimming pool.

'I think it's expensive,' she said, leaning over George's shoulder in the family computer room, while I stood against the wall behind them. 'But you only turn sixteen once, so I know they'll say yes.'

'Must be nice,' George said, scrolling through the website, 'I think for my sixteenth we got Chinese takeaway.'

'We didn't do anything for mine,' Nisha said from the spinning office chair next to us, 'I opened my presents in the living room and I was grateful.'

'That's because you didn't have girls in the class above inviting you to their Sweet Sixteen parties.' Frannie shrugged, 'What am I supposed to do? Not take advantage of it?'

It was true, two girls on the netball team with Frannie had thrown extravagant sixteenth-birthday parties in large venues. I hadn't been invited, but Frannie had, and had managed to convince her parents that she needed one of her own.

'You both got big eighteenth birthday parties,' she went on, 'and I couldn't come to either of them because I was too young. You'll both be at this party, so if you think about it, I'm actually giving you both one extra party than I got. So it's you who can be grateful.'

Neither of them could argue with that logic, especially after George had pulled the website for the venue up on the family computer and we scrolled through the gallery. The four of us huddled around the screen as he scrolled, his fingertips grazing along the mouse. I felt the warmth of his shoulder inches from mine, was painfully aware of the sliver of space between our legs, his long and bent at the knee, in neat black jeans, mine bare beneath my school skirt which was fraying at the bottom. I would often place my hands strategically over the worst of it. At school I was sometimes conscious of Frannie's perfectly pressed uniform, her skirt and blouse taken to be fitted properly and replaced several times during the school year. My own shirt was greyed with age, the blue and yellow tartan of the skirt faded with endless washing. But at Frannie's house I felt none of that. It was as though the beauty of their large house, and their cosy, expensive furniture transferred to me while I was with them. I would often simply forget that I didn't always live here, until I had to go home.

'Do you think we'll be able to use the pool?' Nisha asked, flicking her brother's hands away from the keyboard and navigating across the menu in the header, looking for more information. 'It's not going to be some kind of health and safety rule which means we can't have it open with kids around.'

'There won't be any *kids* there.' Frannie said indignantly, tossing her head so the long sheet of black hair swept back over her shoulder.

Nisha and George shared a teasing glance that they knew would upset Frannie. I knew they were only joking when they did these things, but Frannie would take it personally. This time she made a disgusted noise, got up and stalked out of the room. I made to follow her but George reached out and gently took my wrist.

'You don't have to go with her. Stay with us, she'll come back when she realises you're still here.' If it had been anyone else I would have pulled away and run after my friend, but, feeling colour rise in my face I turned back to him. George got up off the chair and gestured for me to sit down in his place.

'Have you had a proper look at this? It's hard to do anything without these animals sticking their hands in and trying to control everything.' He gestured to Nisha who rolled her eyes and leaned back, opening her new flip-phone and starting to text someone.

'I've got a secret project for this,' George said, 'and I could use your help with it.'

'Yes?' I said, looking intently at the screen, too shy to look directly at him, but knowing that I would do it, whatever it was.

'I'm going to be in charge of the music. That band you two loved when you were kids, the Star Girlz. Do you still like them?'

'We both pretend we don't,' I smiled, 'but if we both had to pick our favourite songs ever, it wouldn't take more than ten tracks to get to one by them.'

'Ha. I knew it. Could you make a list of her favourites for me? I'm going to slip them into the playlist for the party. Mostly because I love her and want to put all her favourite music on there, but also because I want to watch her pretend to be annoyed even though she'll love it.'

He leaned over me to use the mouse and opened a document on the computer called *George Flores Essay Winter 2008*.

'Just anywhere in there for me.'

I scrolled past pages of plans, photos of cakes with lilac frosting, flower-shaped confetti, and a giant star piñata, down to a list of music, most of it pop that Frannie regularly blared while we were in her room. I added the first six or seven tracks that come to mind, inwardly laughing at how quickly I could rattle them off. I could have listed every track, from all four of their albums, in order if needed.

'What are you two doing?' a voice sounded from the hall.

'Nothing.' George said as I quickly saved and closed the document, as Frannie walked back into the room with a drink. She gave us both a suspicious look and, as she set the glass down, George turned to me with a querying expression. I gave him a small nod in return.

Thank you, he mouthed, and we turned to watch as Nisha started to bicker with Frannie for making herself a drink without offering one to me, her *guest,* my heart fluttering with the feeling of sharing a secret with George

*

We sit comfortably in the coffee shop for just under an hour, until George gives a sigh of relief and closes his laptop.

'Productive?' I ask him.

'Very. I'm so glad I could get this all done with nobody bothering me. I love my family but you know what they're like.' I smile and nod in sympathy. 'And I like my colleagues, but it's exhausting, feeling like they all need me all of the time.'

He started to clear up, looking tired. It was so early in the day and already as though his mind felt heavy under the weight of all the things that occupied his time.

'And Rowena is great, but -' he hesitated.

'Rowena?' I ask, thinking I'll know his response.

'My girlfriend,' he says, smiling. Though it's not the smile I would expect someone to make when talking about their partner. It was more like the smile someone makes when reminded of a task they'd reluctantly agree to do.

I don't know what to say, so I busy myself packing away my book and checking my phone. I have a missed call from Frannie and, when I look back up at George, he's staring at his phone too.

'Frannie?'

'Frannie, Nisha, two people from work and Rowena,' he says.

'Well if you don't need to answer any of them right now, maybe put your phone away and we can walk back slowly. Everyone will be there when you're ready for them.'

'I admire your boundaries,' he says, 'I sometimes feel like every thread of me is being pulled in a different direction.'

'I don't think it's boundaries. It's just that nobody ever really needs me,' I laugh, 'I don't know if that's because I don't make myself very available, or if I don't have to be available because nobody ever needs me.

'That is a conundrum,' George says, 'either way it must be nice sometimes to feel like your time is your own.'

He's packed his laptop and papers back into his satchel and, as he goes to put his phone in his pocket the screen lights up again. He looks at it with a tired face and I hold out my tote bag, open by the straps.

'Here.' I say, 'Give it to me for the walk. Then you don't have to feel like you're ignoring people. It's not your fault. I've got your phone.'

For the first time that morning he looks like he's really going to laugh. He drops his phone unceremoniously into my bag and I hear it clunk against my purse. We leave the cafe, calling our thanks to the young woman who moves from behind the counter to collect our cups.

CHAPTER SIX

The day has gone from cool and hazy blue to hot and bright, and I immediately regret not bringing sunglasses as we step out from under the awning, lifting my hand over my eyes to keep from squinting in the sudden, bright sunlight. We walk out across the town square which is now busy with people, sitting out at tables with plates of breakfast or browsing the shop windows. A few children run across our path shouting in Spanish.

'I can't believe how hot it gets here,' I say, 'I feel like Spain isn't so far away from England but the weather is so different at this time of year.'

'Be glad Frannie didn't decide to get married in Jaipur where our other Grandparents live. It's hotter than this all year round. I spent a few weeks there last year and honestly, I don't think I was ever at a comfortable temperature. And of course that's without that lovely snowy skin of yours, which I imagine burns on a sunny spring day?'

'It does, but I've seen Jaipur in Frannie's photos, it looks so glorious. I think I'd happily burn to a crisp to spend some time there.'

'Well if you hadn't been MIA all this time you could have come out with us.'

His tone is joking, but there's a pointedness to the remark that makes me feel uncomfortable.

'Did Rowena go with you all?' I ask, unable to help myself.

'She did,' George says, 'she spent a lot of it indoors under a fan, but she was a good sport about it. She doesn't love the heat'

'Was it really *really* hot?'

'We went in autumn to try and make it tolerable. And it was okay. For most of us at least.'

I do some quick counting. It was spring now. Allowing for the time it would have taken for a couple to do something as big as flying to another continent to stay with family, they had probably been together for at least ten months at this point. I caught myself, feeling childish. It was none of my business.

'Is that why she didn't come with you here?' I ask, 'I don't think it's that hot but I think some people would hate it.'

George seems to catch himself in another sigh. 'No, no. She has work and she's got other things to…' He tails off as we round a corner to a steep flight of stone steps, then turns to me. 'Can you keep a secret?'

I nod mutely as we start to climb the steps.

'I think we're going to break up.'

'Oh. I'm sorry to hear that.'

'Don't be. I think it's time. She's a great person in so many ways. It's just - do you ever worry that the way you love someone makes them worse?'

My first thought is no, but instead I ask what he meant.

'I know I'm a "helper". I can't help it, ironically. I always have to jump in and fix things and make sure people are okay. But I feel like sometimes, with some people, the more you need to help them, the more they become someone who needs help. And I worry that's what's happened to me and Rowena.'

'I suppose that makes sense. I think lots of people

unconsciously change parts of themselves to better suit the person they want to be with.'

'Exactly. We've not even been together a year, and already I think I've become more of a chronic helper than ever, and I'm exhausted. And Rowena has, honestly, become someone who endlessly seems to need help. And she was never like that before. It's like she's endlessly on the brink of a meltdown. We're at a restaurant and she can't find anything she wants and we have to drop everything and go somewhere else. In Jaipur, it was always too hot, too loud, too bright. I spent the whole holiday inside with her. And if that was that person I'd started dating then that would have been my choice. But she wasn't this way when we met. I feel like it's something that's happened as we've been together, and I can't help but feel like I'm making her a worse person by being with her.'

The steps are steep, and he speaks slowly through the effort of climbing them. When he reaches the top he turns around and sees that I have fallen behind slightly. He reaches his hand out and, before I can stop myself, I joke, 'What were you just saying about over-helping? Do you not want me to climb these stairs by myself?'

He laughs, and I see the tension release from his shoulders.

'No you're right, I should work on my flaws. You're on your own kid.' He walks away with comical speed as I climb the last few steps, then slows to let me catch up.

'Why is it a secret?' I ask.

'Because Frannie and Nisha already don't love Rowena. They've been on the end of these little flare-ups, and I don't want them to take this as a reason to speak badly of her. She's a good person and I still care about her. I'm just not sure it's still the right thing.'

'That's very good of you.'

'And they'll just be unbearable. You know how they can be. If they gang up in a moment where I'm wrong and they're right, it can be months of torture. I'll tell them when I can avoid them for a while, maybe a month or so before the wedding so they're both too busy to annoy me about it.'

We walk in companionable silence back to the house. On the path before the turning, we see Lila and the boy from across the , sitting on the curb. He's talking animatedly in rudimentary English, using his hands and staring ahead at the road while she gazes at him.

'Lila,' George calls, and she looks up, her expression that of a small animal caught in torchlight, 'does your mother know you're out here?'

Lila nods. 'She said I can go anywhere so long as I don't bother Paloma.'

'Who's Paloma?'

'*Mi gato*,' the boy says.

'His cat,' George says softly to me.

'I had worked that out, thank you.'

'Sorry.'

We walk past the two children and into the house, where various members of the family are sitting reading newspapers, making pots of coffee or tidying up surfaces. George reaches to start drying pots and is flapped away by an aunt.

'I do wish they'd let me help.'

'Normally I'd admire your commitment to equality,' I say, 'but maybe in your case you should think of it as practice.'

'Maybe that's what I'll do for the rest of our time here.' He says. 'Just not help at all.'

'Exactly. Practice sitting with the discomfort of being

unhelpful.'

'There you are,' Frannie emerges from a back room, 'we thought you'd both been kidnapped.'

'Or maybe eloped,' Nisha calls from out of sight behind her.

'We both went to the same coffee shop by accident.' I say, hoping I wasn't blushing.

'It was nice to catch up,' George smiles, 'without you two yelling over everything.'

The two women protest, but their words mingle together and George laughs.

'See what I mean? How could we talk with this nonsense going on?'

We walk towards them and Frannie smacks him gently in the arm. We join Nisha and Theo where they're sat at the long kitchen table playing cards.

'Hey both.' Theo says.

'Take a seat, I'll get some water.' Frannie says.

George makes to go after her to help but catches my eye. He stops and carefully, deliberately sits down at the table. I sit next to Theo on the other side. When Frannie returns with a pitcher of water and glasses we play cards for a while.

We stay inside during the heat of the day, the five of us sitting companionably in the living room. Nisha has to wrestle Lila away from the front of the house to take a nap out of the sun. Frannie and I curl up together on the squashed white couch with our books, while Theo and George watch a show on Theo's iPad. Nisha comes in with a tray of iced coffee in tumblers and, after giving one to each of us, sits in an armchair in the corner, curls up, and seems to fall asleep in minutes. She looks younger asleep, less stern, her bare feet and ankles tucked up beneath her in the chair, short hair curling around her cheekbones.

George notices Nisha sleeping and reaches out to the iPad to lower the volume slightly. Frannie gives him a thumbs up. I realise it must have been years since I had been with them all together like this in a living room, just sitting companionably, as though I were part of their family. Finally, once the hottest hours of the day are past, it's time for us to visit the church to speak to the priest about the service.

'They've got a beautiful garden.' Frannie says, 'I think we can take some pictures there as well which will be nice.'

I feel warm and sleepy, not made up enough to look good in photos, but I get into a taxi with Nisha and Lila, who can't help but spill information about Camilo in an endless stream to me in the car.

'I don't want you getting distracted by this boy,' Nisha says to her, 'remember you've got an important job at this wedding. If I catch you missing a cue because you're staring at him I'll be furious.'

'Is he coming to the wedding?' I ask.

'The family have known Frannie since she was a baby,' Nisha says, 'they've lived across the way for years. And they've been helpful sorting out some things for the day which we appreciate so they're all invited.'

Lila fidgets in her seat, twisting her fingers in her lap. I feel sorry for her, though appreciative of Nisha's nerves. Lila is too old for any slip-ups on the day to seem cute, and she wouldn't enjoy being embarrassed.

The chapel is a small building set in the mountains, up a long dusty road away from the main town. It is made of the same whitewashed stone as most of the buildings, with wide doors in dark wood, and a little arched cot on the roof, housing a small bell. The windows are set in radiant stained glass that catches the sun as we approach, and green plants climb the walls around the front. When we get out of the car and approach the building, a very elderly man in a priest's vestments and a younger woman in linen trousers and a blouse step out of the door to greet us.

The group speak in Spanish and I allow myself to be led inside. We walk through the chapel, small and quaint, with pews in dark wood and an altar laid in white cloth on a carpeted circle, and out of a door at the back. Through a short corridor, we come to a well-kept garden, bordered by flowering plants, thick with blooms of hot pink oleander, deep purple hibiscus, and asters like giant daisies, turned like happy faces up to the sun. The grass leads through to a paved area framed with narrow cypress trees, on which a small iron bench looks out down the mountains to the sea. I am looking at the bench when I hear Lila shout 'The priest has a pool!' from behind me. When I turn she is gripping the fence of wooden slats at the side of the garden, jumping up and down to look over the top.

The priest, who has walked with Frannie and Theo out into the garden with us, turns to where the girl is shouting, then looks with interest at Frannie, who laughs and translates. Theo, Lila and I are the only people who cannot speak fluent Spanish and look at Frannie, as the priest speaks to her, who then turns to us.

'It was made by a group of people planning to build a big hotel right next to the Church, but the community sent them packing before they built anything else. Now they host children's swimming lessons and aqua aerobics for the elderly every week, and the priest's nephew comes and keeps it clean.'

'Can we go swimming?' Lila asks, turning to Nisha who shushes her. I walk towards the fence to see what the fuss is about and see a large uncovered pool set into an expanse of stone paving slabs, in a jelly bean shape, the water a glittering aquamarine colour.

'Very nice.' George says just over my shoulder, 'Hey Frannie after the wedding we can see which of us can toss you in the pool.' Frannie gives a harsh fake laugh.

'You know it would be such a shame if my brother drowned on the day of my wedding.' Her father snaps his head around and says something harsh in Spanish. Frannie drops her head and mumbles something back.

'What did he say?' I ask George quietly.

'He said not in front of the priest.'

Frannie recovers quickly and gets out her phone.

'Right, I want some pictures. Everyone smooth your hair down. George, you're not getting out of them.' George ignores her, and walks back into the church, putting his phone to his ear.

'Pictures?' Sameera says, 'Why?'

'Because when the wedding comes there won't be time. There will be so many people and we'll be in the chapel then all going back down to the hotel for the reception straight after. We'll have all the photos with the big groups of everyone dressed up, but I wanted to get some pictures of us all together looking more natural, my closest family.'

I feel unsure as she says that, but then she smiles directly at me, as if knowing exactly what would be going through my head, to reassure me that I'm not here by coincidence. She counts me as her family too. I smile back.

'And it would be really nice,' she says, raising her voice loud enough to be heard inside, 'if my whole family would be in the garden for this moment.'

George reappears, holding a bottle of sparkling wine.

'Actually,' he says, as the priest appears from behind him bearing a tray of flute glasses and a glass of orange juice. 'If you can be patient enough to wait twenty minutes, I've actually booked a professional photographer who is on her way up to the chapel and she'll take our photos for us.' Frannie's mouth drops as George smiles. 'I just figured this way you can be in the photos instead of taking them.'

The priest sets the tray down and George fills the glasses with sparkling wine. Lila takes the orange juice and Nisha hands the drinks out to Frannie, her parents, her grandparents, myself, George and Theo. We stand together on the lawn chatting, until we hear the crunch of a car parking on the other side of the chapel, and a young woman in a peaked cap comes timidly round the side to walk in through the fence, holding a large professional camera and a small bag of accessories.

Once the photographer has set herself up and done a few test shots, she begins to direct us. The light from the sun is now low and golden and spills across the features of the garden.

'Just have your conversation for the moment,' she says in thickly accented English, taking a few test shots. 'I will pose you later.'

We do our best to look natural as we continue talking, though we all hold ourselves more carefully, self-consciously checking our hair and clothes as the photographer circles us. The drinks are a godsend, giving us something to do with our hands so we don't fidget. After twenty minutes the photographer begins to gently move us around the garden. Frannie's parents and grandparents are moved to stand by the line of cypress trees. Nisha, Lila, Theo and Frannie are taken to stand beside a spray of large bright oleanders. George and I are left standing together, watching the others being photographed.

'Are we not pretty enough?' George jokes.

'Always the bridesmaid,' I say.

'Me too,' he smiles as he watches the others posing, 'are you having a nice time?'

'It's fun. I've missed your family. Though I feel a bit out of place, I'm the only person who won't be officially in your family once the wedding is over.'

'I don't think that's how Frannie sees it,' he says, 'I think she's always considered you part of the family. We don't see our relatives in Jaipur for a few years at a time, but that doesn't stop them from being our family. It's not a library book, it doesn't expire. If you were part of our family when you were younger, you still are now.'

I'm touched, and want to say something meaningful back, but I'm saved by the photographer coming over and guiding us to our place. We are moved right to the bottom of the garden, where the worn iron bench sits framed by thin blossoming trees and looking out over the sea. The photographer guides us to stand with our backs to the sky as though we've arrived there quite by accident and are just speaking for the first time that evening.

'And just look relaxed together, like you're chatting,' the photographer says.

'Pretend I'm saying something clever and funny,' George says, and the photographer gently tilts her head and guides him to put one hand in his pocket, while he holds up the Prosecco as if gesticulating with the other.

'I don't know if I can act that well.'

He laughs and pulls his hand from his pocket and out onto the bench to steady himself. I laugh in response to his outburst, and nervously tuck a strand of hair behind my ear.

'That's lovely,' the photographer says, 'keep your hand up to your ear and look up at him. Beautiful, absolutely beautiful. You look great together.' With a jolt I realise, she thinks we're a couple.

George has realised it too, and is looking at me, his eyebrows raised as we communicate, silently, that neither of us knows what to do. For a few moments we go back and forth making facial expressions, trying to decide whether we should say something. In the end, we seem to settle on just going with the flow and, with the tiniest shrug, George relaxes back into the pose given by the photographer. After a few photos are taken we are moved in our groups and I am placed in a scene with Frannie, Nisha and Lila, the three adults walk along the patio talking as Lila runs her fingers through the leaves of the aster plants sitting against the low stone wall beside us, her other hand outstretched to her side, as though she is a dancer.

The men are grouped together for a shot, Frannie's parents and grandparents are posed and, by the time we are all brought back together, it is almost dark and the priest turns the lights on inside the church, which sends glowing stripes across the garden. We also realise that the cypress trees are threaded with hanging lights which glow gold as fireflies above us. We take a few more pictures in a group, the photographer directing us to step this way and that around one another, turning and facing the people we pass, as though we're doing an elaborate eighteenth-century dance together. I sense, rather than see, the photographer take a photo as I pass Frannie's mother, and she places her hand fondly on my upper arm, again in the moment in which Frannie and I come face to face and just burst out in silent giggles, as Theo and I give each other a swift high five as we turn past each other like we're on a teacup ride. The photographer shouts that she's almost done as, slightly disoriented, I misstep and move backwards where I collide with someone who turns in time with me.

'Sorry,' I say, as I turn, my hands coming up instinctively to protect myself, straight into George, whose hands come out to steady me and find mine, his fingers curling gently around my own as though we're about to dance. We stand, caught like that for a half-second, our hands together, when a final flash of the camera goes off.

'That's a wrap ladies and gentlemen,' the photographer says in Spanish, as Nisha translates for myself and Theo standing next to her. 'I'll send you the images in the next couple of days, and if you want prints you can let me know. Have a lovely wedding!' We thank the young woman who smiles bashfully, and we all walk back across the dark lawn.

CHAPTER SEVEN

The next day passes quickly. We move from a slow morning and a quiet lunch of bread and oil and orange slices to frantic packing and shouting across the halls. I sit in the living room drinking coffee in comfortable silence with Frannie's mother and grandmother, having packed last night, while the rest of Frannie's family scramble to get ready. It is a familiar experience, the commotion and movement around me while I have quietly already sorted myself out. Staying over at Frannie's house I had always been ready for school or to go home first thing the next day while Frannie argued with her parents over what clothes were clean and where things were. From the outside, it might have seemed as though theirs was a disruptive home, full of conflict. But it was simply the chaos caused by a family entirely comfortable with one another, always happy to speak their minds, with parents who treated their children like people as complex as themselves.

By contrast, it might have looked as though my readiness and neatness were the product of a calm, quiet, harmonious home life. Even Frannie's mother would point to me, standing with my school bag in hand, shoes on and standing by the door and say 'Look, this is a child who was raised right.' Though, as I spent more and more time with the Flores family they understood that wasn't the case.

I am travelling to the airport with Frannie, Theo, Nisha and Lila, taking the same flight as them this time. Before we wheel our suitcases down to the car parked at the hotel, I am wrapped in hugs from Frannie's aunts and uncles and kissed on both cheeks by her parents.

'Shall I walk you down?' George says, 'Nisha you've got suitcases and Lila to look after.'

'She's not a baby, she's carrying her own bag.' Nisha hugs him goodbye in a definitive way. 'Just stay and make sure the rest of the family get on their flights, I'm not rebooking them.'

George shakes Theo's hand, then pulls him into a hug, the two men laughing, then he picks up Lila swinging her around. I wait awkwardly as he turns to me. But he opens his arms and I step into them willingly.

'Let's not leave it so long next time,' he says, his cheek against the top of my head.

'Definitely.' I say.

The hug lasts perhaps a beat longer than it should, though it feels like we're stood together for an age and, when we part and I begin the walk down the cobbled streets of Mijas, I feel the press of his hands lingering where he touched the bare skin of my shoulder. As we cross the street and turn down the path I hear the wheels of Lila's case pause behind me, and turn to see her staring back up the road. Camilo has come out of his house to watch us go, holding Paloma in his arms. Lila raises a small, shy hand to wave her goodbye, and Camilo fidgets with the cat, holding up a little grey paw and waving it back. Nisha calls Lila sharply and she turns again, resuming her walk, and I note the brightness in her eyes, the skip in her step as we walk away from the boy that has so clearly stolen her heart.

London is cold and wet when we return, the clear blue skies of the Spanish mountains replaced with thick sluggish clouds.

'Welcome home.' Theo shouts over the rain as we dash from

the terminal to his car and stash the cases in his trunk, our thin, warm weather clothes soaking through in minutes. Theo drives us all out of the airport, himself and Nisha in the front with Frannie and I in the back with Lila between us. Lila is far less chatty this time, tired from the excitement but also, I sense, distracted by her thoughts. She gazes into space with a dreamy expression as, despite my protests, Theo drives me not to the train station as agreed, but all the way to my front door. I give each of them awkward hugs from where they're sitting in the car and promise to meet them again before the wedding.

'I mean it,' Nisha says with a warning voice, 'you're not disappearing off again, not now we've got you back.' I nod into her shoulder as I hug her, before taking my cases and wandering back up the drive of my home. Jay opens the door before I can ring the doorbell.

'You're home!' he says, stepping back to allow me in, 'we've missed you.'

'We thought you might have caught a bit of a tan,' Adam appraises me from further down the hall, 'but you've just got pink shoulders.'

'I don't tan,' I laugh, 'I just go red.'

They've left the washing machine free for my clothes, and I note as I put away my toiletries and books that they've vacuumed my room and replaced the towels in my bathroom. They've bought me dinner from a local Japanese restaurant, a plate of gyozas and a tub of curry: chopped vegetables, chicken and rice in a glossy, spicy stew. We eat together at the kitchen table as I catch them up on my time in Mijas.

'I had a cheeky look on Frannie's Instagram,' Jay says, 'it looks gorgeous. I've put it down as a holiday destination for next year.'

'It was beautiful,' I say, 'made all the better with the company. I'd forgotten how much I love Frannie's family.'

'And I have to ask, for my own intellectual curiosity,' Adam pulls his phone from his pocket and taps on it a few times, 'who is this?'

He turns the screen and I see a picture of George and I from the night before. We're by the iron bench in the chapel garden, but it's not a professional photo. When I look closer I see that it's a photo shared on Frannie's Instagram, one that she must have taken covertly while the photographer was guiding us into place. I can't tell the exact moment it was taken, but we look as though we're trying not to laugh, as though one of us has told the other a joke in a moment where we both need to be sombre.

'That's Frannie's brother,' I say, 'when we had our photographs taken the photographer thought we were a couple. It was a bit awkward. I think this is the moment we've just realised.

'Well he's gorgeous,' Adam says, 'is he single?'

I shake my head.

'How rubbish. Otherwise, I'd be telling you to call him.'

'It's okay, I've known him since I was a child, it would be strange. We're almost family.'

'Really? I thought you hadn't seen Frannie's family in years. Surely you're different people now?'

'I suppose we are,' I let the sentence fade, unsure what to say. We are different people, but that doesn't mean I can just forget what happened.

'Speaking of family,' Jay said, carefully, 'your father called the landline.'

'Oh.'

'I told him you were away and that I'd tell you to call him back, but if you want I'll just "forget" and pretend it didn't happen.'

I think for a moment, weighing my options.

'No, it's fine. He'll only call again. He's very persistent when he wants something.'

'Do you want to call him back on the landline? Or you can use one of our mobiles?'

'I'll use the landline, thanks.'

'Whenever you're up for it.'

I wait until the next day to call my father back. I have his number saved in my mobile, but I type the number into the handset of Jay and Adam's home phone. The conversation is short.

'We've been clearing out the attic and found some things from the old house,' he says, 'you need to take them to your mother.'

'Can't you just throw them away?'

'You need to take them to her.'

I sigh. If I protest again he'll say the same thing over and over until I'm worn down.

'Fine. Where do you want to meet?'

'I'll meet you in the car park of that shopping centre near here. Where we met last time.'

'Okay.'

'Good.'

We agree on a day and time and he hangs up without saying goodbye.

'How's father of the year?' Jay asks. Adam puts his hand on his husband's arm as though admonishing him, though he too looks at me with concern.

'He's found some of my mum's things in his garage. He wants me to collect them from him in a car park.'

'He won't even let you come over to his house? You have to

arrange a neutral location like you're handing over a hostage?' I shrug, trying to my face with a smile that suggests *what can you do?*

Adam and Jay offer me their car to collect the things and take them to my mother.

'Thank you, though I'll need to try and find out where my mum is living now. She might have moved again.'

Whenever I talk about my family, Adam looks at me with sad eyes and his lips pressed together. He spends every Sunday afternoon on a video call with his large and joyful family who all adore him. His birthday every year involves cards piling up on the mat each morning and opening the door every twenty minutes to a new gift delivery. He is adored, unconditionally, by his family, in the same way Frannie and her siblings are, and cannot understand how someone could experience anything different.

Jay on the other hand understands only too well my experience of a more difficult family. His parents, unable to accept their son's coming out, have cut him off completely. He stands out in their wedding photos, a shock of dark hair amid the ruddy, cheery complexions and coppery blondes of Adam and his enormous family. I remember the first time it struck me that there are no photos of Jay's family anywhere in the house, although Adam's photos line the walls. I wondered if I should have cried, or felt a strong surge of sympathy for him. Instead, I just felt a gentle tug of recognition, for an experience that was not quite the same, but in some ways parallel to my own.

A few days later I borrow their car and drive to the leafy suburb where my father lives with his wife and three children. I don't know which house is theirs, but I take in the size of the homes as I pass through the streets, and huge front gardens filled with toys and trampolines, thinking about the sort of lives people must live in these places. I park on the agreed floor of the shopping centre car park and, as I get out, I see him immediately walking towards me, holding a large cardboard box as though it might ignite at any moment.

'Hello,' he says, briskly, and immediately holds out the box.

'How are you?' I ask, not reaching my hands out just yet. I know he feels uncomfortable around me, and it gives me a tiny, guilty shot of pleasure to draw out the experience.

'Good, good,' he says, casting around for something to say. 'Job's good, all the kids are good.' He stops quickly, and I keep my face impassive as he looks embarrassed and stuck. He does not know if all of his kids are good, because he knows nothing about my life.

'Glad to hear it,' I say. I take pity and hold out my hands, which are quickly stuffed with the cardboard box. It's been hastily taped shut.

'What do your family think you're doing?' I ask. He shifts his feet.

'I told them I found a family of dead mice in the garage, that I was taking them out to a local zoo for the snakes.'

I say nothing, just look at him. My ability to make him squirm just by existing in his eyeline used to make me feel ashamed. Now I don't feel much of anything. We stand for a few moments before he clears his throat, says he has to be going, walks away and gets back in his car, leaving me standing holding his family of dead mice.

When I get home I attempt to call my mother. I ring twice and leave a message during the evening. I don't want to open the box. I worry that if I open the box the belongings will somehow become my problem, and I'll never be able to hand them over. I'll be left with some sad remnants of my parent's long-dead marriage that I can't shift. My father's new family don't know he's been married before, don't know he has a daughter. As far as he is concerned his short-lived first marriage to my mother was a mistake, and I am the unfortunate consequence of his poor judgement.

I put the box under my bed and try to forget about it, tidying my room to take my mind off things. I go to place the French novel I am reading on my bedside table when something slips from the pages and onto the carpet. It's a petal from the rose drink that I had in the cafe with George. It must have fallen from the table and into the book. I flip through to where it had been caught in the pages and see that it has been crushed slightly into the paper, just above a line that reads *"beautiful things should belong to beautiful souls"*, leaving a pale pink mark like a tiny kiss.

Thinking of George I remember the photo Adam and Jay showed me of Frannie's Instagram and I sit back on my bed, pulling my phone from where it sits charging, and bring up her account. She's posted several photos of the holiday, and I swipe through looking for myself and, though reluctant to admit it to myself, looking for George. I linger on a lovely photo of Lila in a white sundress, and one of Nisha asleep in the sitting room, on the creaky armchair, her stern face so vulnerable in sleep. There are a few of me, one in which I'm talking animatedly to Frannie's parents. It's not a flattering photo, I look very pink and my face is in motion, but I'm surprised to see how lively I look, and how warmly they are smiling at me. I see the picture from the photoshoot, in which George and me are fighting off a laugh. And finally, there's another, I almost don't see myself in it at first. It's a photo in which Frannie has captured the beautiful morning view of Mijas from the balcony of her grandparent's house, the same balcony on which we had shared wine the night before. At first, I only notice the beautiful sky, the sweeping landscape, and then I see two figures in the distance walking up the hill towards the house. It takes me a moment to recognise myself and George, and to understand that we must be walking back from the coffee shop. I'm taken aback by the easy intimacy I see between us, despite the time we'd spent apart, despite how nervous I had felt around him. Our arms are almost touching and he's looking down at me, as though listening to something I'm saying. I don't remember anything we had said to one another as we walked back, it felt as though the conversation had flowed organically from us without either of us having to think.

I put my phone away, but spend the rest of the evening itching to look back at the photo. It seems silly and embarrassing, to the point where I leave my phone in a drawer to avoid the temptation. Later that evening I look again as I'm brushing my teeth, I open my phone and the screen is still on the photo, the two small figures of George and I in the distance. Slightly irritated at myself, reduced to staring at a photo like a smitten schoolgirl, I exit from it and find myself back on Frannie's feed. With a jolt, I see there's a new photo, one of Frannie, Theo and George out to dinner with a girl I don't recognise, but realise must be George's girlfriend Rowena. She is pretty and well-dressed, slim with short black hair and a dimpled smile.

Hating myself a little I open up her Instagram and am greeted with a gallery of a life being lived well. Music concerts and dinners in restaurants with high ceilings and stoneware plates. She often has her arm around George, or her mouth planted to the side of his cheek, and captions like *low-key tapas with this one*. I don't know what I had expected. She seems like a nice person, far more sophisticated than I am, a fitting partner to someone like George. In a flash of mean-spiritedness, I try to discern if she's older than I am, closer to George's age, feeling that youth might be the only thing I could possibly have over her. But I can't tell, and I feel guilty for thinking it in the first place. When I get into bed I find the urge to browse through George's feed too tempting. I find him through Frannie's followers. It's a sparse account, rarely updated, with some coffees on tables, books and nice buildings in Europe, but he has the same picture of Mijas and the mountainside that Frannie posted, where he and I are just discernible on the landscape. The caption simply says *Mijas is beautiful.* I notice his girlfriend hasn't liked the photo.

Without being able to stop myself, I wonder what this could mean. I tap my way back to Frannie's Instagram page and look at the photo of them together. With a stirring in my chest, I wonder if George mentioned me too fondly or too often in the days after the trip, or if Rowena sees a look in his eyes in the photos that I don't, a look of affection. The rising tide of excitement I feel at these possibilities is strange and unbidden. I had spent so long worried about seeing George again I hadn't considered the possibility that I would still have all the same feelings I'd had when I was younger. But now I think of us together in the coffee shop in companionable silence, the walk back to the house, the brief moment when his hands closed around mine in the chapel garden as the sun gently slid out of sight behind the mountains, and the way he held me for just a moment longer than he should have when he said goodbye.

I feel in my mind the warmth of his fingers against the skin of my arm and realise all at once that I am in the same place I had been ten years ago. A lost girl, enchanted by someone she cannot have. I think of the line in the book where the rose petal had pressed pink against the page. I do not know if my soul is beautiful, but he is a beautiful thing.

CHAPTER EIGHT

Twelve years ago

I sat on the stairs, feeling the carpet worn rough with age, listening to my mother on the phone. I could hear her voice rising as she spoke to my father, then lowering suddenly to a furious hiss. I had heard these calls before. My father, now married with another child, would be standing outside his home claiming to be on a business call, and would tell my mother to keep her voice down, as though his new wife could sense that the voice on the phone was the predecessor she knew nothing about.

'You know I had to sell my car,' my mother was saying, her pacing restricted to a few steps back and forth by the cord of the phone. 'I haven't been paid, we can't get a taxi. You didn't come to parent's evening again. Not even a card for her thirteenth birthday. This is the least you can do for her, she's still your daughter. Or have you forgotten about her completely?'

I could hear my mother's voice wavering as she spoke. I loved her for speaking up for me, but I hated her for her weakness, her inability to force him to be better for both of us. She had been this way all my life, feeble as an insect wing, as a watercolour painting.

She listened in silence for a few minutes, said 'right' a few times, then, finally, 'Good. It starts at six.' She hung up the phone and took the deep shuddering breath she always took after speaking to my father then turned to me with a slightly forced smile.

'Time to get ready darling,' she said, 'you've got a lift to prom.'

Prom was a strong word. It was a party to celebrate our leaving middle school to attend the local upper school. Almost every child would be going to the same new school in September, but it had been treated by the parents, faculty and the more sociable students as though it were the biggest night of our lives. I had seen dresses girls were wearing, printed out on A4 paper and brought to school, to ensure friends didn't clash colours. They looked like the dresses of Disney princesses. There were plans for tiaras, professional makeup and hair. I took comfort that Frannie wasn't buying into it, so I didn't have to.

'I'll wear a nice dress. I want to look good,' she had said, after grimacing at a puffy mint green monstrosity being shown around by one of the girls, 'but I'm not getting dressed up for this lot.'

With the pressure off I had scoured the local charity shops with a few notes given to me by my mother and had found a pretty dress in a pale, silvery blue with thin straps and a skirt that flared into a gentle circle around my shins. It was ever so slightly too big, but I found that a few carefully placed safety pins helped it sit properly against my narrow, childish frame.

After my mother had convinced my father to collect me, I went upstairs and pulled it on. The pins didn't work as well as I'd remembered, and, as I tried to brush my hair, the nerves of the evening created an uncomfortable twisting feeling in my stomach. My mother came in and told me I looked beautiful, and dabbed a pot of pink cream blush on my lips and cheeks. She braided a thin blonde strand of my hair and tied it with a clear elastic, running a cotton pad around my fingernails, neatening up the teal nail polish I had applied clumsily that morning.

'I don't feel good,' I said, the knot in my stomach seeming to tug at my insides.

'You're just excited,' my mother said, 'you'll feel great when you're there. Don't be nervous. You'll have an amazing time and I can't wait to hear about it.'

My father's shiny silver car parked on the road and waited with the engine running. I stepped out in Converse trainers that my mum had painted silver, holding a little plastic clutch purse, and walked towards the car. My father greeted me gruffly as I got in the passenger seat.

'Right, remind me where this school is,' he said. I detailed the directions and he puffed out his cheeks as the car pulled back out and drove away. 'That's miles. It feels like it used to be closer.'

'It was.' I said quietly. We had to move out of the town centre, to the outskirts where we could afford to live.

The twisting feeling in my stomach was getting worse. I pulled my arms around myself as we drove and pushed them gently into my lap to try and stop the cramping. I'd never felt excitement like this before, or nervousness, no matter what my mother had said. The feeling was growing into genuine pain, as though something inside me was being wrung out, as though parts of me were coming loose and dropping away. With a sudden horror, I realised what was happening, comprehending the alien feeling of something being released in my body and starting to pool beneath where I was sitting.

I started to stammer, trying to work out how to tell my father what was happening.

'What?' he said, and when I stared at him in horror, 'you look like you're about to throw up.'

'I think-' I said, trying to get the words up and out of my throat when everything else in my body was sinking with shame. 'I think I've started-'

'No,' my father said, 'no you're not, not in my car. Lift up.' I pulled myself awkwardly up in the seat. My father looked quickly and groaned. 'For god's sake. Stay lifted up, try to hold it in.'

'I can't,' I said, mortified, 'I don't know how.'

'Well sit on your hands,' he said, in a nasty voice that made me feel awful, 'don't get it on my seats whatever you do.'

I tucked my hands beneath myself as we drove, until he swung the car into a petrol station and pulled the brake so hard I jolted in my seat.

'Go and sort yourself out,' he said.

'I don't know what to do,' I said, 'it's my first one.' For some reason, I couldn't name what was happening to me. As though it was a dirty swear word that would offend my father. He already looked offended. He pulled his wallet from his pocket and stuffed ten pounds into my hand.

'I don't know. Just go in and ask if they've got something. Ask if they've got a bathroom you can clean up in,' he paused and then handed me another ten pounds, 'and get some car wipes, or just kitchen wipes.'

I got gingerly out of the car, as I glanced back I could see a smudge of red on the car seat where I had sat.

'What am I supposed to tell my wife?' he said, more to himself than me. He put his head in his hands and groaned as if I was ruining his life. I closed the car door and walked away, trying to hold my bag behind myself while still walking normally.

As I entered the petrol station I saw that four young men were standing by the fridges where the beers were kept. One had already opened a can and was drinking from it deeply. I walked a few steps into the petrol station, edging towards the toiletries, where I could see a small pink pack of sanitary towels, thinking of the pack my mother had brought two years ago for this exact moment, which had sat gathering dust in the bathroom ever since. As I approached the aisle, one of the men swore and shoved the other and he fell back against the glass of the fridge. I turned and ran back outside. I walked towards my father, to ask him to go in for me. He was stood by the car his phone to his ear.

'I know darling, I know. But this meeting is important. You should see the idiots I'm dealing with.' I stopped walking towards him. Then I threw his money on the tarmac, running down the street away from the petrol station as fast as my feet would carry me.

After a few minutes of running, I stopped, my chest heaving, my stomach roiling. I could feel blood beginning to stick to the insides of my legs. Marks on my dress were now visible against the pale blue fabric, but I was too upset to care. Out of breath, I looked around. I was in a small neighbourhood not too far from the school. It would have been a twenty-minute walk, but I couldn't face it. I would arrive with a blood-soaked gown and, I realised, tear stains on my face, as my chest tightened and my eyes stung. I sat pathetically on the curb, and thought of my father, wondering if he'd realised I was missing yet. I envisioned him finding the money and panicking, wondering if I'd been kidnapped. Would he be frantic with worry right now? Or would he be in his car wondering if a problem had been lifted from him?

Without me, he could simply leave my mother in his past, I realised. He could have the life he wanted, with his new wife and his new baby, without being tied to his past mistakes. I sat for a while, the evening getting darker and colder around me. My father had never been affectionate, had always had a difficult relationship with my mother, at least as far back as I could remember, and when he had first left I had foolishly wondered if this new chapter was a chance for us to have a better relationship as a parent and child away from a marriage that hadn't worked. But I had been wrong. I huddled, making myself small sat on the curb. I pulled my knees tight towards me and rested my head on my forearms, feeling the full force of what I had sensed for some time, but was only just coming to accept. That my father did not love me. Did not want me. Did not even care about me the way I felt that most people should care about one another.

I wrapped my arms around my knees, biting my lip and digging my short bitten fingernails into the flesh of my upper arm as tears slid down my face. It was a few moments before I realised that someone was softly saying my name, and I looked up into a face that I knew, though not very well yet. He had been eighteen then, his hair cut very short and his face still soft with youth, in a dark leather jacket, beneath it a shirt and tie that I recognised as the sixth form uniform of the upper school.

'Frannie's friend, right?' George asked. I had never really spoken to him before. A few pleasantries at the table when staying at Frannie's for dinner, comments about a TV show we both liked when it came on. It was mortifying to be suddenly seen like this by anyone, let alone the big brother of my best friend, who I knew very little about, other than that he was good-looking and funny.

I nodded, wondering if I could somehow disappear from existence, and have him forget he'd ever seen me.

'What are you doing out here?' he looked at my dress, 'Shouldn't you be at prom? I've just dropped Frannie off. I can give you a lift too if you like?'

The simplicity of the offer, the small unthinking gesture of kindness, was too much and I burst into tears again. George watched awkwardly for a few moments, unsure what to do, then it seemed to dawn on him that something was missing.

'Where's your mum?' he asked, 'Or any adult. You shouldn't be out by yourself.'

'My dad was supposed to take me, but I - something happened - I ran away.'

'Ran away? Here,' he took his phone out of his pocket, 'do you know his number? I'll ring him, he must be worried about you.'

'No.' I said, too quickly to avoid suspicion. George looked at me with worry.

'What's happened?' he asked. And when I didn't answer. 'Hydie, you can tell me. Whatever it is, it'll be okay.'

He sat beside me on the curb as I spoke. I watched his face turn from polite interest to concern, to disgust.

'He didn't come in with you? He didn't help you?'

'I got blood on his seat.'

'Who cares?' George scoffed, 'You can't help that. I think when Frannie started her period my Dad went out and bought us all hot fudge sundaes. It was great. Actually, now that I think about it when Nisha was about your age we all got cupcakes one day for no reason.' He reflected for a moment. 'Anyway, here,' he got up, 'let's not sit here on this curb. Do you want to come to prom? I can drop you off.'

I looked at my hands. 'I've ruined my dress.'

'I can take you home?'

I felt my lip tremble at the thought of going back. Of explaining to my mother how I'd been let down. Of seeing her face fall.

'Okay,' George said, his voice completely calm and understanding, 'new plan. Come to ours. Frannie and Nisha have stuff you can use. I'll let our parents know and they can take you back later.'

I nodded. He stood up and extended a hand down to me.

'But your car seats.' I said, feeling my face burning red.

'You can sit on my jacket,' he said, then, when I started to protest, 'it's fine. I promise.'

I took his hand and he lifted me gently to my feet. He took off his jacket as we walked to his car parked on the other side of the road, a small boxy red hatchback, and laid it over the passenger seat.

'Get in, it's fine,' he said, as I stood awkwardly at the passenger door. I clambered in, tucking my dress in a pile beneath me to try and keep his jacket undamaged, and we drove away.

In the car, George asked a bit more about my father. I explained to him the situation as best I could. That my father had left me and my mother four years before, that he had a new wife now, and a young baby boy. And that the new family did not know that he had an ex-wife and a daughter.

'That's mad,' George said, 'I thought the worst thing would be a parent who left and never saw you. But this is somehow worse. A parent who leaves and then pretends you don't even exist?' he shook his head. 'Awful.'

I didn't reply, just held the soft fabric of my dress like a safety blanket. We pulled up to the drive I knew well and walked up to the house. 'Nisha's at university. My parents are out for dinner,' he said, 'so you won't have to talk to anyone.'

Inside, the house was quiet and warm. George turned the lights on and guided me to the upstairs bathroom and, while I looked in the cupboards for sanitary products, knocked and passed a folded pair of pyjamas and a plastic bag through a just-opened door.

'Put your clothes in there for the moment and leave them in the bathroom,' he said. 'Mum says she can wash everything with some special stain stuff when she's back, I just phoned her. So don't worry about it.'

The pyjamas were a sweater and full-length trousers in a soft fuzzy fabric, navy with stars and moons. They were slightly too big for me, and I felt like a child in them. I splashed my face with water, trying to fade the teary streaks down my face that looked so bright and raw in the light of the bathroom. I padded back down the stairs and found George standing in the living room.

'Take a seat. I wasn't sure what would make you feel better,' he said, 'but Frannie and Nisha usually have some combination of these.' He nodded down to his arms, in which he was just about holding a bottle of water, a box of painkillers, a hot water bottle and a large bag of chocolate buttons. I took the water and the painkillers.

'Not the chocolate?'

'I feel bad taking them.'

'Well, to be completely honest, I want them. So why don't we open them and you can have some if you want?'

We sat on either side of the couch with the chocolate buttons between us, and George put on a rerun of a show we both liked, one we often defended when Frannie badmouthed it. I took a handful of the buttons and lay my head on a cushion, putting them in my mouth one by one and letting them melt, dark and sweet across my tongue, feeling the tension leaving my body. At some point I had fallen asleep, waking for a moment when a door opened and shut, and then again to see Frannie's mother Sameera laying a blanket over me, tucking the hot water bottle into the crook of my arms. I was comfortable and warm, as though cocooned, and then I was woken properly by loud voices somewhere else in the house. Frannie was standing at the door to the living room, looking out towards the front door. She looked beautiful in a simple burgundy dress, her long hair in a ponytail, but her body was set, like she was standing guard.

'Frannie?' I say, lifting myself up to sit on the couch, 'How was prom?'

'Boring without you,' she said.

'Who's talking?'

I stood up to join her, and she put out a hand to stop me standing in the sight of the doorway. Peering around I saw people in the hall. I realised that my father was standing at the front door, his phone in his hand. George was facing him, his voice loud and angry. Between them was Frannie's father, his hands out and placating both sides.

'Your Dad's mad George took you here without telling him,' Frannie whispered, 'and George is mad because your Dad is a piece of shit.'

'And your Dad?'

'I think he's trying to make sure nobody gets punched.'

We listened to the altercation. I turned away from the door and stood very still, as though if I moved, I would be seen by my father, pulled by my wrist through Frannie's family home and dragged back out into the night. But after a while the door was closed, hard, and I could hear only George and his father talking in the hallway.

'I'm not saying you're in the wrong George,' his father said, his Spanish accent hushing the G's into H sounds, 'but you should have left me to talk to him.' George said something back that I couldn't hear, and then I heard his footsteps hard on the stairs as he disappeared. Roberto said a few quiet words to his wife then followed George upstairs.

'You'll be staying with us tonight,' Frannie's mother said, coming into the room, 'I've called your mother and she's happy for me to bring you back in the morning. I haven't said anything else, it's not our place, but I can come in with you to talk to her if you like.'

I nodded, the relief at knowing I wouldn't have to go back with my father like a warm haze in my body. Frannie ran upstairs to put her pyjamas on while her mother sat me back down on the sofa. She brushed my hair, as she often did when I came to hers with it in thin tangles. I could hear the rumble of the washing machine in the background and knew that she had already put my dress in to wash, no questions, no judgment. Sameera put my hair into a loose braid to sleep in, saying it would keep my wavy hair protected for the morning and called gently up to Frannie, who shouted back loudly that she had changed. She gave me a soft kiss on the cheek and looked at me in a way that she often did, a sad smile that made me feel cared for, but also pitied. I climbed the stairs and entered Frannie's room, clambering into the sleeping bag and blankets that she'd laid out for me.

'I don't know what George gave you,' she said, 'but if you need anything else for your period there's loads in the bathroom.'

She put a boxset tape of *Friends* into her bedroom television, and I lay quietly in the dark listening to the familiar sounds of the cast's voices in the background, as Frannie began to talk about the party that evening.

After an hour Frannie had fallen asleep, and the episodes buzzed in the background as I lay on the floor. In gaps between episodes, I heard the sound of Frannie's parents talking quietly downstairs, the rumbling of the washing machine, sounds of normal domestic life, a life I had never quite had. As I drifted into sleep I thought of George, his dark eyes concerned for me, the passionate anger as he spoke to my father, the warm skin of his hand as he held my fingertips. I thought of all these things and felt something within my heart flutter awake.

CHAPTER NINE

I try to ignore my phone as I get ready for work the next day. It takes all of my willpower not to check social media again, like a scab I want to pick at. I brush my teeth, wash my face and dress, paying close attention to myself the whole time, trying to anchor my thoughts to the present moment, so they don't drift. Adam and Jay call goodbye to me from their bedroom as I leave the house, and I realise it's a Saturday. The underground is quiet and, as I walk towards the shop, I take happy note of the warm air of spring turning to summer. Absentmindedly, I open my Instagram and realise the app has not refreshed, that I am still on Frannie's profile.

I go to close the page, trying not to look, but something catches my eye. The photo of George and Rowena at dinner is gone. I check again once I'm back above ground and walking along the road to Meticulous Ink, wondering if the lost signal on my phone has caused the app to glitch, but no. I refresh several times and find the same thing. The photo has been deleted.

As I approach the glass doors, I see that they are unlocked and open, ten minutes before opening time, and know that Graham must have arrived. I put my phone into my bag and push the thoughts from my mind. He greets me as I walk inside, calmly raising a hand in a pressed white shirt.

'How was sunny Spain?' he asks, 'You haven't got much of a tan'

'I don't get a choice to tan. It's either come back the same or come back bright red.' I say, finding it funny that Adam and Jay had noted the same thing.

We exchange light chatter as we unpack the boxes for the day ahead. We are barely into May, but Back to School is already on the cards. We put new deliveries of academic planners, bound in navy and bottle green with smart foiled text, onto the shelves. I take handfuls of new pens over to the wall, carefully placing each into its home as though introducing a new member of the family. They sit in their pots like happy flowers as the daylight pours through the glass doors.

To my surprise we have customers as soon as we open, several young women who compliment the window display and run their hands along the notebooks like they are shopping for dresses. I watch them out of the corner of my eye, how they test the bright pink and pastel pens carefully, discussing what would be best for their planners. They are young and lovely-looking, each dressed for the summer a few weeks early, with shiny hair and tote bags full of second-hand books they must have bought from the charity shop at the end of the road.

They each buy a notebook and several pens, and one of them buys a pack of gold metal bookmarks in pretty patterns. Graham makes them laugh with a friendly discussion about his granddaughter, who is about their age. As they leave I notice one of them turns and, framing it carefully, takes a photo of the storefront before they leave.

The rest of the morning is busy, but a lull falls over the street at noon, and when Graham goes to lunch I get time to tidy the shelves, wipe down the sills beneath the window displays, and check the notebooks for sun damage. When I've finished tidying the wrapping paper behind the counter I turn to face the door and, to my surprise, see Lila running in towards me. I almost don't recognise her with her long hair tied into a plait, wearing a pink sweater and white jeans. She calls my name and runs around the counter unceremoniously, flinging her arms out towards me. I catch her in my arms and give her a hug.

'What are you doing here?' I ask, and she looks at me like I'm an idiot.

'We came to see you, obviously,' she says.

'We?'

I look up and see George, leaning against the doorframe. My heart jumps like I've been electrocuted.

'I hope you don't mind,' he says, 'I'm looking after Lila while Frannie and Nisha are getting the dress altered. They mentioned you work a few tube stops away so we thought we'd drop in on you.'

'Not at all, it's lovely to see you both,' I say, 'I didn't think I'd see you again until the wedding.'

George also looks different, away from the sun of Mijas, though no less handsome, in a black jacket and plaid blue shirt with jeans and brown boots. Where in Spain he had looked incredibly Spanish, sun-kissed and tipped in gold, here he looks quintessentially London, just missing a takeaway coffee cup in his hand.

'It's beautiful in here,' George says watching Lila run around the store with wide eyes, 'are you on your own?'

'I'm with Graham, he's on his lunch break.'

'Have you had yours?' George asks.

'Not yet, I go second. I like a shorter afternoon.'

'Well if you fancy a walk, Lila and I were going to have a stroll around the park up the road. The internet tells me there are swans and Lila's starting to find me boring. I'm hoping I can save her from a swan attack and get her affection back.'

'From what I hear swans can break a man's arm, so you'll

need all the help you can get. She'll be very disappointed if she watches you lose a fight to a bird.'

'You're right, I'll probably need backup. I'll buy you a coffee to say thanks.'

When Graham returns from his lunch I introduce him to George and Lila, and walk down the steps to the staff room to get my bag and jacket. I wish I was better dressed. I'm in a pair of cropped grey jeans that I'm never sure flatter me, and an oat-coloured jumper that has become a little stretched through wear. I try to arrange my hair more neatly on my shoulders in the staff bathroom and fish out some mascara from my bag that I touch to the ends of my lashes. Oddly I had relaxed back into George's presence when he was in front of me. What made me nervous was the spectre of him conjured by my memory, and the strange parasocial effect of seeing someone on social media. When he's in front of me, he's as human as I am. No less beautiful, no less lovely, but a person I can respond to, rather than an ideal that lingers in the memory of my childhood.

I walk back upstairs to the shop floor, where Lila stands on tiptoe on one side of the counter, Graham on the other. He's sliding something into a small paper bag and, when he tells her the price, she hands over a crumpled note. Graham hands back a few coins and the parcel. Lila clutches the paper bag to her chest with one hand, while handing the change to George.

'Thank you,' she says, and I realise she is sheepish, as though slightly embarrassed by her purchase.

'You're welcome.' George says, pocketing the coins. He looks around as I approach.

'Ready?' he asks.

'Ready.' I reply, and the three of us wave goodbye to Graham and walk out into the street.

We wander through a few residential streets to a nearby park, a wide stretch of grass, dappled with sunlight streaming through the canopies of trees that grow on either side of the wide path that cuts through. The day is warm and bright and full of birdsong. As we walk, Lila shouts and points into the trees, and we look up to see starbursts of bright green flitting between the leaves.

'The London parakeets,' I gasp.

'I always forget about them,' George looks up at the birds, 'it's like a little surprise every time you see them flying around between the pigeons and squirrels.'

'It's one of those local mysteries isn't it?' I say, 'Where they come from?'

'I think the consensus is that someone's pet birds got loose sometime in the seventies and multiplied,' George says, 'I like that line of thinking. We always think that past mistakes cause future problems, but in this case, it's like a past mistake has made the future world a tiny bit more beautiful.'

We walk to a small wooden hut selling pastries and hot drinks.

'So what do you get when rose lattes and matcha aren't on the menu?' George asks as Lila picks out an apple juice and a gingerbread figure wearing a carefully floral dress.

I ask for a cappuccino, which is handed to me by the barista in a brown takeaway cup, and George pays for it on his phone while I'm opening my coin purse.

'You don't have to do that,' I say.

'You're here on swan patrol with me,' George says, 'I'm just compensating you for your time.'

He also pays for a flat white for himself, and a small paper cup of peas available from a tiny freezer behind the barista, while Lila explains to me at length that bread makes the water dirty and gives ducks stomach problems, and that peas are the best thing to feed them. The park is more crowded than I would have expected, with Londoners taking advantage of a beautiful day to spend some time outside. A few families with small children gather near a cluster of swings and see-saws in bright colours. George asks Lila if she wants to join them, but all the children are younger than she is and she rolls her eyes at him before running a few feet ahead to see the ducks moving serenely through the water of the lake.

'Honestly, how could you even ask that?' I tease George, who puts his hand to his forehead in mock distress.

'I don't even know. World's most stupid uncle clearly.'

'I think they do mugs with that on, you know?'

He laughs, and I feel lightened and happy.

'Can you keep a secret?' he asks.

'Probably?' I say, a wary question in my voice.

'It's nothing bad, but since we spoke in the coffee shop that morning in Spain I've done some thinking.'

'Right?'

'I've broken up with Rowena.'

'Oh,' I stop, wanting to say something meaningful, then default to the cliché, 'I'm sorry to hear that.'

'It's not really something to be sorry about. We'll both be okay, nobody's to blame. We're just not right for one another.'

'That's very mature,' I say, 'I think it can be easy to cling on to things like that, and just decide not to look too hard. But facing it head-on and making a decision is definitely better than leaving it to get worse.'

'You think so?' he turns to me, 'I'm glad you feel that way. I've always thought you were wise about these things.'

Again I'm not sure what to say. He knows my 'wisdom' about relationships comes from my upbringing, but I don't want to raise something that will make me seem like someone in need of sympathy. I'd left that life behind and tried not to think too hard about it. I cast around for a line of conversation that will take us away from me.

'I saw a picture of you two out with Frannie and Theo on Frannie's Instagram last night. Then when I went back on the app this morning it was gone,' I say, 'I wasn't being weird, ' I say hurriedly, 'I just happened to still be on the profile.'

'I asked Frannie to take it down,' George says, 'I said Rowena didn't like how she looked in it. Truthfully, I ended things the morning after that, and it felt crass to let that photo stay up.'

'You didn't tell Frannie?'

'I haven't told anyone,' he says, 'that's why I asked if you could keep a secret.'

'I won't say anything,' I say, 'but why not?'

George sighs and takes a sip of his coffee. We both turn our heads to where Lila is throwing handfuls of frozen peas into the water where the ducks are gathering, jostling for a spot.

'I think it would just be a distraction for my family while we're all supposed to be focusing on Frannie and Theo and the wedding.'

He looks at me, and I cross my arms.

'And?'

'And I'm just not quite ready for them to say they told me so yet. Not until I can tell them over text and then just avoid them for a month.'

'Very brave.'

'I know. It's not my finest moment, and I'll tell them before the wedding. In the meantime, if you could just refrain from telling anyone, I would appreciate it.'

'Your secret's safe with me. Though why did you tell me?'

George looks at me, with an expression I can't quite read, but before he can speak Lila runs back up to us, breathless and bright-eyed.

'There are so many ducks,' she says.

'And I bet they're grateful for their lunch,' George said, 'we should see about getting some of our own. How long do you get Hydie?'

I check the time on my phone. 'I have about half an hour, but I always let Graham go home early so he won't mind if I'm ten minutes late.'

'Great. Let's find somewhere to eat on the way back.'

We walk together, and as we leave the park Lila runs to put her juice bottle and the empty paper cup into a bin. She runs back to us and, with both hands-free, runs between us and takes one of ours in each of hers. George gives her an indulgent smile, as though she's the most important person in the world. As we walk I see, out of the corner of my eye, George lower his head to kiss Lila softly on the back of her hand.

We find a small sandwich shop, the exterior painted buttercream yellow, the interior a little cramped with wooden tables and blue floral tablecloths. The elderly woman at the counter makes us each a sandwich and wraps it in wax paper and we take them to sit down at one of the tables.

'What did you buy at the shop Lila?' I ask, and am surprised when she becomes coy, shrugging her shoulders and taking a large bite of her sandwich.

'Don't be shy.' George says, 'She met him too, remember? You can tell her.'

'It's a secret.' Lila says. George looks around and lowers his voice.

'I already told Hydie a secret to keep for me today, so I know we can trust her.'

'Really?' Lila looks up at me and narrows her eyes. 'What was the secret?'

'Well, I can't tell you that, can I?'

Lila studies me for a moment, then decides that was the right answer. She rummages in her small rucksack and pulls out the paper bag Graham packed for her.

'I'm going to write a letter.' She says, laying out several sheets of beautiful shell-pink writing paper, embossed with golden foiled stars. The paper is accompanied by a small pack of envelopes in a light rose red.

'That's beautiful. Whoever receives that letter will be very lucky.'

'Are you going to tell Hydie who you're going to write to?' George says.

Lila turns pink and tries to stop the smile coming onto her face.

'Camilo.'

'The boy with the cat in Spain?' I ask, remembering his messy chestnut curls, his thin legs in dusty sandals.

Lila nods and gathers up her things.

'Lila doesn't have a phone, obviously, so she asked if she could send him a letter before she goes back to Spain.' George says. 'It's incredibly cute.'

We finish our sandwiches while George teases Lila gently about Camilo. His jokes take me back to when I had been a child watching him tease Frannie about crushes on boy band members. He had always known the right button to push to get a reaction without being cruel. Frannie had laughed and feigned anger in the same way Lila does now, and it's as though time is reversing and I am a child again, feeling my insides turn to dappled sunlight in his presence.

George and Lila walk me back to the stationery shop. I go to wave them off but Lila jumps up and flings her arms around me. I crouch to hug her back.

'I'll see you soon okay? Good luck writing that letter.' and when she lets go George steps up and opens his arms. I step into his embrace and, like last time, there's a beat when each of us should let go but don't.

'See you soon,' George says, stepping away again, 'look after yourself.'

'You too.' I say. I watch them walk away until they round the corner to the tube station. I feel a sudden cold drop on my cheek and look up at the grey clouds as I step back into Meticulous Ink, realising that we just missed the rain.

CHAPTER TEN

I borrow Adam and Jay's car the following weekend to drive to my mother's flat, after finally getting hold of her to find the new address. Before setting off I carefully place the the box my father gave me on the passenger seat. I haven't looked inside it, though the evening before I allowed my curiosity to stretch to shaking the box gently. It rattled, lots of small items sliding around one another, I could have guessed. My mother has always been a magpie, and something of a hoarder, storing piles of tiny glittering things like a dragon.

Her new flat is in a sad grey building with narrow windows, and I have to walk up the flights of stairs beside the broken lift. When I knock she takes a few minutes to open the door, but when she does she flings her arms around me and I breathe in the familiar smell of her patchouli and jasmine perfume, worn for so long that it's baked into her pale freckly skin, her wild curly blonde hair, and everything she wears. The strength of the scent transports me to the tiny house we had lived in before my father had left us, the art supplies and pottery everywhere, the times I had pretended to be asleep in bed, listening to the arguments downstairs.

'How are you my darling?' she asks. The flat is cramped and cluttered, though it's not the flat's fault. It happens to every environment my mother occupies for more than a few moments. The fraying mauve couch, sagging with wine-coloured cushions and embellished throws, hulks in the centre of the room like a huge sleeping animal. The surrounding space is occupied with footstools and rugs, odd little figurines and lamps, stacks of books, candles and oil burners. I would live in constant fear of my mother burning her home down if she didn't always lose her matches.

She's set out a plate of biscuits and a pot of tea for my arrival, and I navigate my way onto the sofa which groans as though I've bothered it while my mother flits around the room. I pour tea into the chipped mugs, unsure what of she's doing. She seems to be shifting piles of belongings from one place to another.

'I bought the box,' I say, trying to find a way to get her to settle.

'Oh,' as though she had forgotten I was in the room she blinks up at me, then returns to the couch. 'Oh, I don't know if I want that, Hydrangea, it must be things from so long ago.'

I try not to wince at the use of my full name, a name that only she ever calls me. Even my father hated it.

'I don't want them,' I say, 'I need you to take them. I won't be able to do anything with anything in here.'

'What if some of it's yours?' she says.

'It won't be. It'll be earrings and perfume samples and tea lights. You might find some things you've been looking for.'

I know I'm being unnecessarily brisk. My mother is complicated, but not unkind, and when my father finally left us she took care of me as well as she could. It was hard being the child of two people so thoroughly unsuited to being parents, but I had happy memories of my mother. My father had guarded his spaces jealously, locking the door to his study while he was in there, ordering me away from his vinyl collection and his model cars. My mother, on the other hand, had always had an open door for me to join her in her passions. All her pots of paint were mine to borrow, all the clay she had used to make vases for art fairs had scraps rolled into balls and stored for me to play with. After my father had left she saved doggedly to buy another Star Girlz magazine subscription for my birthday, working at a museum gift shop while trying to sell her crafts at weekend art fairs, while my father had begrudged every penny I cost him. I take a deep breath and find, beneath the impatience, the kindness I feel for my mother.

'I would like to look through the box with you,' I say, 'there might be things from my childhood here.'

Her face softens and she goes through to the kitchenette to look through the drawers for scissors. When none appear she goes through to the bedroom she uses as a craft room and reemerges with a box-cutter. I lean back as she slices through the masking tape sealing the lid shut. We open it together. It's largely as I expected, bundles of sequinned scarves, a wind chime, a packet of incense sticks that now smell mostly of must, and a deck of playing cards that have been stained by coffee or tea being dropped on them.

'Anything you want?' I ask. I know full well my mother will keep everything in here, will absorb it back into the mass of objects she surrounds herself with. She's been this way for as long as I can remember, and I wonder sometimes if all this fabric serves to absorb the echoes of loneliness I know she must feel. She seemed lonely when she lived with my father, lonely when she was raising me, and now she lives alone and doesn't see me that much, she must be lonelier still. She never talks about friends or dates or places she goes. Her life revolves around pulling things into her orbit and never letting them go.

'I'll go through it this evening,' she says, sifting through the box, then gives a cry of delight, 'Oh Hydrangea look at this.' She pulls out a wonky pink box made of thickly painted clay, shaped into a five-pointed star. 'Do you remember this?'

I don't remember it at all, but looking at it I realise I must have made it. It's the shade of pink I would always gravitate towards in my mother's paint pots, and the top is decorated with roughly made clay shapes that are just about recognisable as moons, dolphins, daisies, and other images I remember from the Star Girlz magazines.

'I made this?' I say, taking it carefully from my mother.

'When you were little,' she coos, 'oh you were a sweetheart, so creative. You were going to give that to Frannie for her birthday remember?'

I privately feel relieved that I'd obviously given Frannie some other, better gift for whatever this occasion had been, looking warily at the patchy paint and poorly applied glitter glue.

'Are you going to take that home?' she asks, 'It might be nice on a dressing table.'

I cannot think of a room dark enough to store this, so I go to hand it to my mother for 'safekeeping' but as I go to lift it I feel something slide inside the box, from one end to the other. Though I don't know what it is, and have no memory of putting anything inside it, I instinctively pull it back and place it gently into my bag.

'Yes, I'll take it back with me.'

I sit on the couch for another half an hour, while my mother moves restlessly from one place to another, slowly finding space for every other item in the box, returning now and again to the couch to take a sip of tea and a bite of biscuit, like a hummingbird dipping into the nectar of a flower for a few moments before taking off again. When I leave I'm exhausted, just from watching her inability to sit still, and make excuses soon after eating dinner with Jay and Adam to go up to my room. The box in my bag, with its secret contents, sings to me while I get ready for bed, but I wait until I'm in my room, sitting cross-legged on my duvet, to take it from my bag and examine it.

It's not as ugly and poorly made as I had originally thought.

Away from the background noise of my mother's flat, I can see the paint is slightly shimmery, which hides the worst of the patchiness. The star is formed with care, each point shaped into a soft rounded tip. I shake it gently side to side and feel something inside, again, sliding with the movement. The lid is stiff, stuck with age, and I worry I'll break it but I prise it carefully off and set it to the side.

There, sitting on top of a yellowed envelope, is my Star Girlz charm bracelet, the one I had thought lost long ago. I lift it with my little finger and each of the charms swings slightly on the chain, as if coming to life. A moon, a star, a daisy, a silver heart, a music note, a dolphin, a feather, and at the end, the faux opal set in silver. Frannie's birthstone that I had swapped with her.

It isn't the full collection I had once had. I had lost a few, and some had been left at the house I'd lived in while my parents were married. The divorce had been quick and cruel, so a number of my childhood belongings had been lost to my little bedroom in that house, with its peeling wallpaper and plastered ceiling. I wondered sometimes about the stuffed cat I had had, the plastic dinosaur I found in a Happy Meal and kept on my bedside table, the boxes of colouring pencils and Jacqueline Wilson books that I had adored. I nurtured a faint hope that, though it was unlikely, my father had taken them to a charity shop where they had been bought by the families of other children who would love them. But he had probably swept it all into the bin, like he had tried to do with most of the things connected to that time in his life. It gave me a cruel satisfaction that occasionally a box of old things would materialise in his attic or shed, all these years later, his old life rising from the grave.

This, however, is my old life, looking at me. Each little motif attached to memories of Frannie, of school friends and dance routines and flashes of a smiling older boy who always stopped in the kitchen to say hello while I was doing homework at his kitchen table. Out of pure curiosity, I peel the envelope out of the box. At first I assume it's an old utility bill or school report, something I grabbed off a table to line the box. But the front when I turn it over is blank, and opening the flap, I see that it's a handwritten letter. When I pull it out I almost drop it to the floor. It's a letter I had written to George, maybe a year before I had confessed to him, back when I was seeing him almost every day. I recognise my very best handwriting, painstakingly laid out in blue fountain pen. I had decorated the top with a sheet of holographic star stickers. As I look at it I experience a strange phenomenon. Before opening the letter I had forgotten that it had ever been written, and yet the moment I begin reading I realise that I still know it by heart. Like the lyrics of a beloved song that has been forgotten suddenly playing on the radio.

I had agonised over every word, thinking so carefully about how I could best express my feelings. Wondering how I could possibly say everything he meant to me in something so limiting as words. I read the lovelorn sentences of my past self, expecting to cringe, but instead I feel sympathy for her, and maybe even admiration for writing something so deeply personal and raw. I would never allow myself to be so earnest now, even in a private letter. I also realise that the George I had known then is almost exactly the same as the George I know now. Someone who was kind to a fault, protective and loyal to the people he loved, slightly self-conscious and self-deprecating, clever and ambitious while never losing the gentle side of himself. And I realise, as I read the words I had written over a decade ago, that everything that made me love him then, still makes me love him now. I don't want to admit it to myself, to peel away the protective mask I had laid over those feelings. But there they are, as though they had never really gone away, and all of a sudden I feel clammy and sick, the rush of emotions I had pushed down are overwhelming and I clutch the bracelet like a talisman, the edges of the charms pressing into the flesh of my hand.

I'm not ashamed or embarrassed to feel that way about him. In fact, it seems bizarre to me that everyone George meets wouldn't see him as I do. But I recognise the problems that my feelings could cause. I jeopardised my oldest friendship because of these feelings. I have altered my life in ways I can never take back. Because of these feelings, I gave up a home that felt like a sanctuary from the turbulence of my own life, and here they are again, as strong as they have ever been, and I don't know what to do about it.

CHAPTER ELEVEN

In the weeks that follow I ruminate on my feelings, trying to untangle the adolescent crush from the adult friendship we had formed, to work out where one ended and the other began and somehow split them apart. And would then find a silly video or interesting article in my social media messages, sent from him, and would have to respond the way a normal person would. As though receiving a tiny sparkling reminder, every few days, that we were not only friends, not only on good terms, but that he actively thought about me, thought I would find things interesting or funny and wanted to share them with me, wasn't sending me into a tailspin.

And the hardest part of this experience was that I still didn't know if he remembered. I was enjoying my best friend back in my life, and rediscovering George as an adult, building a friendship that I had missed out on for years, with this gnawing unanswered question in my mind. I considered asking him now and again, wondering about ways to slip it into our intermittent text conversations, but I couldn't. There is simply no good way to ask someone: 'Do you remember that time I told you I loved you?'

I go over to the Flores parents' house one evening after work, for dinner with them and their children. Lila is visiting her father, Nisha tells me as she takes my coat.

'Does he see her much?' I ask as we walk through to the dining room together.

'Oh plenty,' Nisha says, her face neutral, 'he's a good Dad, he was just a bit of a rubbish partner.'

We walk past the kitchen where Frannie and her father are squabbling over a cooking pot, a cloud of steam seeping out from under the lid, and join her mother and George at the kitchen table where they're drinking mugs of tea.

'Darling!' Frannie's mum says, getting up and embracing me.

'Hello trouble,' George smiles. I try to grin back normally, forgetting which muscles make what facial expressions.

'How is everyone?' I ask, 'I heard Frannie and Roberto having one of their more civilised conversations.'

George laughs and Nisha rolls her eyes.

'I swear,' she says, 'they shouldn't be allowed in the kitchen together. It's literally an argument over whether you drain boiled rice with a sieve, or you put the lid on the pot and tip it so the water comes out of the steam hole.'

'And of course, they're both wrong.' Sameera says, shaking her head, 'If either of them were capable of measuring rice properly it would soak up the water perfectly and they wouldn't have to drain it at all.'

'A half-Indian girl who can't cook rice.' George shakes his head. 'Honestly Mother, where did you go wrong?'

'The worst thing is there's going to be loads of this horrible soggy rice left over,' Nisha says, glaring at George, 'and it's all your fault.'

'What do you mean?' I ask.

'Rowena was supposed to be coming too,' Nisha says, 'but apparently George forgot to tell her and now she's busy.'

'Ah.' I look at George and raise my eyebrows. He waits until the two of them have turned their heads away before giving me a knowing smile.

We have a secret again, George and I, as we did when compiling Frannie's birthday playlist, and like last time I feel a quiet exhilaration from it. After dinner, we help clear up, and I find myself in the kitchen with George as we empty and reload the dishwasher.

'Think they're buying it?' he asks, as I hand him forks to put away in a long drawer beside the sink. The edge of his thumb grazes my hand as he takes the cutlery from me.

'Nobody seems any the wiser,' I say, 'do you think you'll keep up the charade for long?'

'I'm just waiting for the right moment. I need some more excuses, I need things to happen that are important enough for Rowena to not be able to attend things, but not so important that my parents or sisters will message her.'

'We can brainstorm a few,' I say, 'car breaking down is a no-brainer. Maybe a minor running injury?'

'She doesn't run, but she does do pilates,' he says, 'what do you injure doing pilates?'

'What are you two whispering about?' Nisha says, coming in to wipe down the placemats.

'Just asking Hydie about work,' George says, while I flounder, 'I told you, didn't I? Lila and I visited Hydie at work a few weeks ago.'

'Yes, she bought that letter-writing kit.'

'Has she written the letter yet?' I ask.

'She's not even put pen to paper,' Nisha says, 'she keeps saying she's still thinking about what to say. She won't tell me who it's for, so I can't even help.'

I had sympathy. My own letter to George had been a painstaking effort, and even when it had been finished it had felt silly, which is why I had never given it to him. I wonder privately, as Nisha and George continued talking, what would be in Lila's letter. Whether she would pour her heart out as earnestly as I had. She was only eight, I had written my letter when I was fourteen, but I knew how keenly a young girl's love was felt. The ghost of it lingered in the moments I caught George's eyes over dinner, or when he put a hand in the small of my back to brush past me in a doorway.

'Remind me. Why did Frannie delete the picture of you if she doesn't know?' I ask George quietly, as Nisha leaves the kitchen to find her sister.

'I said Rowena didn't like the way she looked in it., George shrugs, 'a lame excuse, but it's what I've got.'

'It is pretty lame. I don't know her but she didn't seem like the self-conscious type.' I can't work out why I'm keeping Rowena in the discussion. It's as though I need reassurance, just a little more, that George is now single, that I am not having these feelings about a taken man.

'Oh?' he gently tosses the dishcloth across his shoulder and turns to face me, 'you got any better ideas?'

I feigned being deep in thought for a few moments.

'She's actually a government agent and has just left for a top-secret mission. She has to hide her whereabouts the night before she left so nobody could trace her.'

'Oh that is convincing,' he says sombrely. I notice him biting the inside of his lip to keep from laughing.

'Or maybe that the dress she's wearing is one she borrowed from a famous celebrity and hasn't returned. If she's photographed in the dress the celebrity might see and start hassling her for it.'

'Now that one could actually be true,' George breaks his serious character and laughs, 'I've got a couple of sweatshirts

I've realised I might never see again.'

'There you go,' I say, 'everything adds up!'

He smiles, but it falters as he looks at me.

'Sorry,' I say quickly, 'I shouldn't make jokes, it's only been a month. Are you feeling okay about it?'

He frowns slightly, as though assessing his own emotional landscape, but then his face relaxes and he smiles again.

'I'm sad to say goodbye to someone I cared about. But I'm also relieved. I've known we weren't right for each other for a while, and every day I didn't say anything I was both lying and wasting her time. It was the right thing to do for both of us.'

'Frannie's right,' I say, 'you are too nice.'

George just looks at me quizzically, so I continue.

'People don't talk about breakups like that. They make the other person out to be the villain, or a crazy person they had to get rid of. Even if the break up was the right thing to do, people say things they don't mean while the wound is still fresh. How are you so lovely even now?'

George thinks for a moment, seeming genuinely stumped by my question.

'You know what?' he says, 'I think it's partly because of you.'

'Me?' I say, put out in return by such an unexpected answer.

'Yes. I remember when you were younger.'

My heart leaps in my chest as I wonder if he's going to bring up Frannie's birthday, my confession. I'm not ready. I don't know what I'll say.

'I know you had a tough childhood,' he says, 'and I know we didn't talk about it much, but I remember rescuing you from that curb when you didn't go to prom. I remember all the times Frannie would tell me that you didn't know where you were going for dinner, or were left standing at the gates because your parents didn't communicate about who was meant to pick you up.'

I can't keep eye contact, I look at the ground, slightly ashamed that he would talk about something so openly when it made me so vulnerable.

'And I felt so angry on your behalf,' he says, 'you know a couple of times me and Nisha would discuss you just coming to live with us. Or going over there and just telling your parents what we thought about them, both of them, the one that fucked off and pretended you didn't exist, and the one who wouldn't pull herself together enough to care for you properly. Our parents shot us down the one time we mentioned it to them but I know they were concerned too.' He pauses, shakes his head.

'I hated them for you Hydie. But you were never unkind about them. You never complained. You always tried to see the best in your mother, even though she always let you down. I don't know how you feel about them now, but it made an impression on me.'

He steps forward and, in a movement that seems almost unconscious, places his hand over mine where it rests on the kitchen countertop.

'It made me realise how lucky I was, how lucky I still am to have good people in my life. Even when people hurt me, or leave my life, I think on some subconscious level I still think of you, in your frayed school uniform at our dinner table, eating the first hot meal you've had all week, talking about how your mum painted your favourite flowers on your bedroom door. And I try to see the world the same way you did. The way I think you still do now.'

We stare at one another in silence for a few moments, but Nisha and Frannie walk back into the kitchen bickering about the entertainment value of a reality show, and as though waking from a trance, George and I come back to ourselves and finish tidying the kitchen, while his sisters pour glasses of wine and continue talking as though nothing has happened.

I stay late at the Flores' house. Roberto and Sameera say goodnight and the four of us gather in their living room and I sit on their long deep sofa, Frannie lounging across and putting her legs affectionately in my lap. George and Nisha each take a squashy armchair on either side of us. The TV buzzes low in the background as we chat. The noise is mostly Frannie and Nisha discussing the wedding. As she talks Frannie lifts her left hand above her and turns her wrist, so her engagement ring glints in the light. The way it catches the light sparks something in my brain.

'Frannie, I found my Star Girlz bracelet last week.'

She stops and lifts herself up on her elbows to look at me.

'No way. Did my Mum tell you she found mine? I won't get it now but she found it in a box of school things. I thought I'd lost it for good.' She lolls her head back and I can tell that the wine has made her slightly tipsy.

'God, I loved them so much,' she says, 'I still listen to them sometimes. On a bad day, I'll blast that song *Meet Me At Midnight*, and think about my party. Do you remember? When we were kids, and it came on and we all went mad and rushed onto the dance floor?'

I remember, but I can only give a stiff nod. I see a blurred sliver of George in my peripheral vision and, though I don't dare look across, I swear I can feel his eyes on me.

'It's funny,' Frannie continues, 'I think back on that time and I can't believe how things have changed. I swear it was five minutes ago and we're all completely different people. Well,' she glances at Nisha, 'most of us.'

Nisha scowls at Frannie and inadvertently looks so much like her grumpy teenage self that the rest of us burst out laughing, and after a few moments she relents and joins us. We laugh until creaking from the room above us reminds us that their parents are asleep. We check the time and realise that I've missed the last train home. I start fumbling around on my phone to book a taxi, but Frannie gently takes it from me.

'Just stay here,' she says, 'you can sleep in my room.'

'Is there space?' I ask. Though their house is large, Frannie as the youngest always had the smallest room. I could fit on the floor beside her single bed as a child, but even as a teenager, it had become cramped.

'Sure there is,' Frannie says, 'If you sleep on the bed, I'll curl up on the floor next to the wardrobe.' Even as I picture it I can see that Frannie lying there would put her at least partially sleeping under the bed.

'Better solution.' George says, he looks tired, rubbing his eyes with the heel of his hand. 'Hydie sleeps in my old room and I bed down here on the sofa.'

'That works.' Nisha says clapping her hands matter-of-factly.

'I don't want to kick you out of your room.' I say.

'It's not a problem,' he says firmly, 'I'll just come up with you to get pyjamas and a pillow.'

The four of us troop upstairs, the mother in Nisha kicking in as she insists on pouring each of us a large glass of water. She and George go into their rooms while I follow Frannie to the bathroom. It's been redone since I was last there. It had been done in dark blue tiles with shimmering marbled streaks of silver and teal. I had often pretended it was an enchanted lagoon. Now it's been redone with decor in eggshell pink.

'There'll be a spare toothbrush somewhere,' Frannie says, digging in the cupboard beneath the sink of their bathroom, 'Mum always keeps a stash for when we forget them when we stay over.' She stands up with a small plastic capsule which she clicks open and unfolds to reveal a small toothbrush. 'Her only rule is you have to take it back and use it. Otherwise it's wasteful. We keep them for travel, so you can bring it when you come to Spain again.'

I take it gratefully and borrow the skincare in the travel bag she and Nisha keep on the windowsill to wash my face. The bag of serums, creams and toners sits beside small tubes of face wash and moisturiser that are in the gunmetal grey of men's skincare.

'Is that George's?' I ask.

'It is,' Frannie says, 'If we did one thing right as sisters it's getting him using skincare. And Theo borrows it if he ever stays over. No man in my life goes un-moisturised.'

When we're finished we step out of the bathroom to where George and Nisha are waiting. They've both changed into pyjamas, Nisha in a camisole top and shorts, George in a soft white top and navy sweatpants. Nisha holds out a bundle for me.

'It's an old top of George's,' she says, 'you won't get much from old sleeps-in-her-pants over there.' She nods over my shoulder to Frannie.

'Aside from nightmares if you happen to be getting a drink while she walks to the bathroom.' George mutters, grinning and ducking as Frannie throws a washcloth at him.

'Thank you,' I say, before crossing the hall to George's room.

'Make yourself at home,' he says in the doorway as I stand awkwardly on the carpet clutching the shirt I have been given, 'it's all clean, I washed them last time we stayed here.'

He holds a hand out. 'Just one thing, try each of those pillows and whichever one you like least throw over here.'

I press into them gently, deciding they are identical, and pick up the one closest to me and throw it underhand across to George who catches it deftly.

'Thanks,' he says, 'If you need anything give me a shout.' And when I nod he says, 'No really, if you need anything, ask *me*. Nisha is an appalling person when she's just woken up, and Frannie will be basically naked.'

I laugh and he reaches in to close the door.

'Goodnight,' I say.

'See you tomorrow, trouble.'

The door closes softly and I hear his footsteps creeping softly back downstairs.

I didn't see George's bedroom much when I was a child. I spent most of my time in Frannie's room listening to music and painting my nails, or occasionally creeping with Frannie into Nisha's to go through her makeup and jewellery. My abiding memories of George's room were slices glimpsed through a door left just open: Blue wallpaper, a wooden desk piled high with homework, video games and sports magazines, and a single bed made up with a bedding set covered in red and blue dinosaurs.

The room is different now, the walls are the same pale blue, but the wooden desk is tidy, with just a small pile of books and a hooded jacket draped over the chair. The bed is now a wide double, and the bedding has been replaced by something sombre and slate grey. Something in me is sad that the bedding has been changed. There was something so endearing about the thought of George, fifteen, then seventeen, then twenty years old, still curling up to sleep in the bedding he had slept in as a little boy. I change quickly, incredibly aware of undressing in someone else's house, someone else's bedroom, and then I gently slide into George's bed in just his shirt and my underwear. It feels bizarre to me, even though the sheets are cold and the bedding is slightly stiff, having clearly not been slept in for weeks at least. I lie awkwardly on my back with my hands holding the top of the sheet like an old lady clutching her purse, almost embarrassed to make myself too comfortable. I replay the conversations we had in the evening, the sudden, unexpected rawness of the things he said in the kitchen. We had been laughing, trading jokes, and then all of a sudden he had become so sincere that it had felt intimate and uncomfortable.

I wasn't sure what to make of it. It had been flattering, I suppose, to hear him say that I was such an influence on him, but to hear him discuss my childhood out of the blue had left me feeling exposed. Perhaps, I consider, he was just saying these things because he was feeling emotional. However stoic he was being, he was still fresh from ending a relationship with someone he had cared about. Someone who would have been there that night if he hadn't chosen to break it off beforehand.

I realise as I think this, that if Rowena had been there, it would have been her and George sleeping up here, with me relegated to the sofa. I try not to think about it too much. I fail. I wonder if talking about her tonight brought back memories of evenings spent here together. I wonder if they too had shared jokes in the kitchen, shared drinks on the sofa with his sisters, and dug through the bathroom cupboards for toothbrushes. Had they made gentle fun of Frannie's refusal to wear pyjamas and Nisha's grouchy moods? And instead of George saying goodnight and going downstairs, had they gone together into this room and shut the door behind them? I try not to think of them curling up in this bed. I hold no ill will towards Rowena, am aware that I have no right to feel jealous or upset at the thought of her and George together, but still, the thought tugs at my brain, sags over me like a raincloud. I turn off the light and lie in the dark, feeling very alone, haunted by the spectre of someone else's relationship. And then I hear the gentle tapping at the door...

CHAPTER TWELVE

I expect to see Frannie at the door, some late-night gossip she has to share, or Nisha checking if I need more water. But instead, I open the door halfway to find George standing on the landing. The half-light in the hallway falls against his face, carving out his cheekbones and jawline, picking out in silver the tips of his lashes, the curve of his upper lip.

'George?' I say, as though he might not know his own name. He takes a step towards me and pushes the door just wide enough to come through. I instinctively take a step back, and he moves to fill the space, stepping into the bedroom and closing the door quietly.

'Tell me if you want me to leave,' he says. I say nothing.

George reaches out and cups my face in his hands, thumbs tilting my chin up as he leans down and pushes his mouth against mine. For a moment I am too stunned to kiss him back, but then something inside me takes over. In silence, I lift onto my tip-toes and slide my hands up his chest until my arms cross around the back of his neck. George moves one hand down the side of my body, settling on my hip as the other gently lifts my hair behind my shoulder as he moves to kiss the side of my neck. I feel entranced as his mouth moves against the tender skin, feeling the pulse in my own body as it quickens in response to his touch. It is as if I am dreaming, as if I have conjured some kind of apparition of George to fill the gap in my heart where I would have him, but then his teeth graze sharp against my shoulder and I know he is completely real, pressing against me and pushing me gently towards the bed. I go with him, walking backwards like we're ballroom dancing until my legs touch the bed, and then I am leaning back, my arms still around his neck, pulling him down with me. Then he is above me, looking down at me as though he too can't quite believe we're here.

His fingers drag slowly to the hem of the shirt I'm wearing, his shirt I realise, as he looks at me with a questioning expression. I respond by lifting my arms so he can gently pull the shirt up and over my head. Suddenly topless the gravity of the situation hits me, that I am undressing with George in his parents' house, while his sisters—my friends—are asleep in rooms nearby. I wonder if I should stop George, if I should protest, but then he leans back and pulls off his own shirt, his deep skin taut across well-defined muscles, and as he crashes his mouth back into mine, I forget that there is anybody else in the universe.

Our movements turn frantic as our breathing gets quicker. George's fingers move down to the waistband of my underwear and pull them roughly down my legs, throwing them off the side of the bed. I go to do the same to his sweatpants but he takes my wrists forcefully and pins them back up by my face.

'Keep them there,' he whispers in my ear, and I obey as he moves down my body to sit between my legs. He parts my thighs with his hands, and I watch him lick his lips as he lies with his head between my legs. As his tongue slides against me, I hiss between my teeth and have to cover my mouth to keep from moaning. He's good, moving his whole mouth against me as though he's eating sweet, ripe fruit, his tongue pressing rhythmically against my clit, and his hands holding my legs firmly apart. I twist my hands into the sheets from the pleasure of it, trying not to cry out, my breath coming in sharp gasps as I buck my hips against his jaw. The pleasure rolls like a tide, each wave getting stronger and stronger and I push him away before I can finish. He looks up at me, his eyes dark, his mouth shiny with wetness. He crawls up the bed, his eyes fixed on mine and then he is kissing me again, pushing his tongue deep into my mouth, filling me with my own taste. I press the length of my body against his, feeling how hard he is. My fingers go to work pulling the waistband of his sweatpants off and he writhes out of them.

Suddenly we are completely naked together on the bed. He toys with my hair where it sits against my collarbone, his other hand rubbing a thumb lightly down my breast. The moment is like a spell, and I hate to break it, but whisper in the dark.

'Don't we need-' George smiles and extends an arm over me to his bedroom drawer.

'This is my room remember,' he says, 'I've got some hidden in the back here.'

A few moments later he is ready. He puts a steadying hand flat against my lower belly.

'Sure you want this?' he says, giving me the smile I have always loved.

'Yes,' I hear myself, breathless with need.

'Sure you're sure?'

'Yes.'

He leans forward and I feel him push hard inside me, my body stretching to accommodate him. I cry out at the slight pain, and he puts a hand over my mouth to keep me quiet as he begins to move. He starts controlled, like he is finding a rhythm, focused on being pressed close against me and I loll my head against his shoulder holding my breath to keep from crying out as he moves faster and faster inside me. I feel my own wetness sticky against my inner thighs as he pushes himself up and adjusts himself to sit back on his shins, leaning back with my legs around his waist, his hips slamming against me. I watch his eyes roving across my breasts, my waist and hips.

He presses his thumb in hard steady motions against my clit, watching my face for my reaction. I try to keep my face dignified but the intensity of the sensation, his cock hard inside me and his fingers against my clit coupled with the effort of keeping quiet are too much and I feel myself squirming beneath his touch, as though I am both trying to escape, and trying to get more contact than physics allows. He smirks, pleased with himself as he watches me, my hair now damp against my forehead, my whole body at his mercy beneath him. I feel him torn between feeling his own pleasure and causing mine, but he doesn't have to wait long, the dual sensation builds like a storm and suddenly there is thunder and lightning as I shudder, my whole body tensing and releasing. With the last moment of effort I have left I lean up and catch his mouth, our lips and teeth clumsy against one another as his breath begins to hitch and he fucks me hard. He grabs the back of my neck and buries his head in my shoulder, muffling the shuddering moan as he finishes inside me.

We lie together in the dark, our skin damp where our bodies touch, both breathing hard. George turns his head and kisses me on the cheek, and I turn to do the same, my mouth touching the soft velvety skin of his temple.

'So…' he says quietly against my face, 'Come here often?'

I snort with laughter and he shushes me, his own face creasing with suppressed laughter.

'Hydie, people are sleeping, have some manners.' He pulls me towards him and holds me, both of us shaking with the effort of not laughing out loud.

When I wake George has left. I had fallen asleep in the crook of his elbow. Part of me had wanted to stay awake, to talk to him, to find out everything I had missed in his life in the years of being away from him. But after we had cleaned up and pulled our clothes back on we had slid into bed and slept like a couple, tucked up together beneath the sheets. I have a vague memory of his lips gentle against my forehead as he pulls away from me in the dark, the door opening and closing softly, and then my eyes open and light is streaming in between the curtains and I hear the unmistakable sound of the coffee machine brewing downstairs. I pull on the clothes I wore the day before, feeling very conscious that I have not been able to shower and that I am wearing the same underwear that George pulled off me. After I have run my fingers through my hair to try and neaten it and dressed as best I can, I stand holding the handle of the door.

I could run into George on the landing. Or find him asleep on the couch still. Perhaps he will look embarrassed. Perhaps he will tell me it was a mistake and we should act like nothing happened. I stand stupidly on the carpet looking at the door, as though there is any way I can avoid finding out.

Eventually, a voice calls up the stairs. It's Frannie, and I have to leave the room. The landing and stairs are free from anyone as I walk down into the hallway and to the kitchen where I find Frannie standing at the kitchen counter, the smell of hot coffee filling the room.

'Morning,' she says brightly, 'did you sleep okay?'

I try to scan her tone for any extra meaning, but can't sense any.

'Pretty well thanks,' I say, then, unable to resist, 'it took me a while though. How did you sleep?'

'Like a log,' Frannie pulls a second mug from the cupboard above her and swaps it in the machine, pressing the buttons again. 'It's the same every time I stay here. Something about my childhood bedroom makes sleep so easy. It must be something psychological. Like I can shrug off all the stresses of adulthood. Is oat milk okay?'

'Fine thanks. Where are the others?'

'Mum and Dad are already out for breakfast if you can believe it. George has jumped in the shower and Nisha is still asleep.' She pours milk into a mug and hands it to me. 'And if you try and wake her she'll maul you like a bear, so let's not be too loud.'

We sit around the table quietly drinking coffee and looking at our phones for a while. When we're done Frannie offers to drive me home. I try to insist on getting the bus, but she shushes me irritably as she walks back into the kitchen.

'Of course, I'll take you. We can leave whenever you like.' Frannie says as she rinses our cups.

'Now is good,' I say, quicker than I mean to. Frannie looks round, surprised.

'I just have errands to run today. You don't need to rush, just whenever you're ready.

She shrugs and picks up her jacket, and we leave the house while Nisha and George are still upstairs.

'That was fun,' Frannie says when we are in the car. 'Reminds me of the old days, except there's alcohol and gossip now, instead of Capri Suns and homework. And I forgot how well you and George get on.'

'Oh?' I say, keeping my tone neutral.

'Yeah. I missed you two together. You were the only ones who could make fun of me and I didn't mind.'

I force a polite smile and look down at my phone, pretending to be absorbed in a news article. I'm tired. I must have only slept for a few hours at a time, and my head is spinning from the night before. Even if I had wanted to speak to George I couldn't have done it there, not in front of his family. But perhaps I should have tried to catch him on the stairs, to address the situation. But instead, I had scarpered before seeing him at all, and I wasn't sure that had been the right thing to do.

Frannie makes another attempt at conversation, and I pull myself together and we talk about our jobs, and make plans for a holiday sometime in the next year.
'Obviously, the honeymoon is expensive but I would love to do a staycation sometime. Just a little rented flat or a Bed and Breakfast somewhere, you and me, or maybe us, Theo and siblings? What do you think? Hydie?'

It hadn't occurred to me that after Frannie's wedding, it would be expected that I would continue to have a relationship with her family. That in Frannie's eyes our friendship had been restored to its original closeness. I felt the conflict of all the love and gratitude I felt to them all, for all their kindness towards me, and the uncomfortable feelings that had resurfaced around George, made all the more painful now that we were adults, made all the more confusing now we had slept together.

'Hydie?' Frannie says again, and I hear the hurt in her voice.

'Sorry, I'm just a bit tired and distracted,' I push away my thoughts, angry at myself for not being attentive to her. 'I would love that so much.'

I pull up my phone and search for coastal getaways, and we spend the rest of the trip talking about locations around the borders of the country.

When I get back to Adam and Jay's house I slump inside. They've already left for whatever social activities they have planned, and I go up to my bedroom and allow myself to fall into bed, my tiredness pulling me into sleep before all the negative feelings are able to catch me.

It occurs to me in the moments between sleeping and waking, the moment where insight so often happens: If George remembers so much about me from when I was young, if he had thought about me in that much detail, and retained it all in the last ten years, he must surely remember Frannie's birthday. And if by some miracle he had forgotten, Frannie had mentioned it the night before. I will sleep to take me before the implications all fall into place, but they catch me just before, a kaleidoscope finally turning in a way that puts the pieces together and I realise - It is almost impossible that George does not remember the last moment we spoke. The moment I told him I loved him.

CHAPTER THIRTEEN

In spite of everything, the shame creeps back in over the next few weeks. It's not shame that I have slept with George, but shame that this memory is still hanging over us. With the realisation that he must remember, comes the old fear, back to haunt me.

I leave it longer and longer to reply to Frannie's messages and find reasons to turn down the next three invitations: a cinema trip with the siblings, drinks after work near Frannie's office, and a barbecue at Nisha's house. I wonder if George will message me, but he doesn't. I wonder if I should message him. I don't. I sit sadly on my bed on the evening of the barbecue, staring at the rain sliding down in thin streaks across my window, hoping the clouds haven't reached where Nisha and Lila live, just out the other side of London. I feel miserable and stupid, but equally I feel helpless to do anything better. It's as though I willingly choose the dull, aching pain of missing out and feeling alone, so I don't risk a sharper, keener sting.

I go down and join Adam and Jay, who are having a rare evening at home. I approach tentatively, never sure how welcome I am with them when they're having time together in the house, but they smile and make space for me on the couch. Adam gets up and makes me a cup of milky tea.

'Are you okay?' Adam says, 'It's nice to see you. You've been out more than us the last few weeks.'

I try to give a neutral shrug. 'I just fancied a night in.'

They're watching a reality TV show in which lots of very beautiful people engage in a merry-go-round of relationships while sequestered in a luxurious beach house. I try to stay engaged, but I have trouble keeping up with everybody's tangled relationships. As my eyes close, two women in string bikinis exchange gossip about a man with carefully styled hair, and then all of a sudden I'm waking up on the couch with a blanket placed over me.

The world outside the windows is dark, and the lights have been turned off, all but the small lamp in the corner of the room, which Jay, who would have gone to bed after Adam, must have kept on for me. I fumble my hands along the arm of the sofa and the low side table next to it until I find my phone and flip it over to check the time. I'm completely taken aback by the stream of notifications I have from a number I don't recognise. I open my phone to the chat and see a wall of short texts.

Hydie!! Are you coming tonight?

It's George by the way x

Forgot you won't have my number! Well here it is, let me know if you need a lift or anything.

Then a few hours later:

Frannie says you're still not feeling well! Sorry to hear that, get well soon. Maybe we'll have to all come to yours and have a sad evening on the sofa with you.

And another couple of hours before the last messages.

Frannie says you're not answering her texts much any more. Is everything okay? She'd never ask but she's worried about you.

I stare at this strange wall of messages. George has never messaged me before in my life and suddenly he's plastering a wall of texts on my screen, while conveniently not mentioning the obvious point of conversation between us. I catch myself gnawing at my fingertips as I scan through them a second time, guilt building at the thought of Frannie, who hated looking vulnerable, confiding something like that in her brother. I quickly type a response to him.

Everything's okay! I feel better, I just needed an evening to rest. I'll give Frannie a text tomorrow morning, and if I've forgotten, give me a nudge!!

The text sends and, less than a minute later, a reply comes.

You're up late.

I realise I didn't take in the time when I turned my phone over. I look properly and realise that it is just past midnight.

So are you!

Wow, these messages are embarrassing to read back. I promise I wasn't drunk this afternoon. Unless you can get drunk on lemonade and hot dogs.

I reply.

It's fine. I promise everything's okay, I'm just not always great at checking my phone.

Like this evening?

I was asleep!

That explains why you're awake now.

What's your excuse?

Good question. Just a bit wired from the barbecue. Promise everything's okay? I know we probably need to talk at some point. But I didn't want to chase you.

I type a few iterations of a reply. Attempting to say I'm fine without making it seem strained or insistent. In the end, I delete them all and simply reply: *Promise.*

Good. If anything's ever the matter I'm here for you. Hopefully we can talk soon, it's sucked not having you around again.

I stare at my screen. I feel unsettled. I know I've been pulling back, but I'm uncomfortable with being so confronted over it. Nobody has ever cared where I am.

I try and nonchalantly change the subject.

Thanks. The only thing the matter now is that I didn't eat dinner, I'm starving!

Oh no! What do you have that's appropriate past midnight?

I walk in my bare feet to the kitchen. At any other point in the day, the fridge is a dream, full of fresh vegetables and cheeses, two pizza doughs ready to roll out and cook and Tupperware full of sauce for the slow cooker. But at 00:15, seeing nothing that can be shoved straight into my mouth makes me sad.

Nothing :(I might have to cook something from scratch.

Oh no! Don't do that!

I'm typing that I don't mind cooking when the next message comes through.

Fancy a nocturnal adventure?

An adventure?

I know somewhere that will make a delicious dinner, even at this time of night.

Where is it? Can I walk there?

It's a bit of a way, up by Richmond.

Ahh I don't know if I can the tube all the way there

He sends a face rolling its eyes.

I'll come and get you genius.

A minute later I'm creeping past Adam and Jay's bedroom to my own, dressing in a lilac dress that laces at the back and brushing my hair and debating makeup. I settle for some mascara and tinted lip balm and then I'm standing by the door like a teenager waiting for the headlights of George's car to round the corner of the road. He's later than he said he would be, and I spend a few minutes thinking he's fallen asleep, or decided not to come, but then I hear tyres on the gravel and open the door to see the front of a sleek gunmetal car coming to a halt with its front wheels on the drive. I slip out, touching the keys, money and phone in my bag to be sure I have them, and close the door as gently as I can. I approach the car and the passenger side opens.

'Fancy meeting you here,' George says from the driver's side.

'Right? What are the chances?' I get in and stuff my bag awkwardly down between my feet. George restarts his car and it moves smoothly away from the drive and back along the road.

'I'll drive you back afterwards,' he says.

'Where are we going?'

'One of my favourite places.'

'Not cryptic at all. You know that's what a murderer would say.'

He looks offended, though he's still grinning.

'You think I would come all this way for something as pedestrian as murder? You think very highly of yourself.'

'Maybe it's revenge for not messaging Frannie back.' I say, then immediately realise I shouldn't have. George spots the open door and pushes on it.

'Yeah what's up with that?' he says.

'Nothing,' I reply, 'I was just busy, that's all there is to it.'

'Sure,' George says making a sceptical face, and I sense I've only earned a reprieve, and that I may have to trade this food trip for an actual discussion about the last night we were together.

We drive through the quiet London suburbs. George parks

in a narrow street with low, red brick buildings. On one side is housing, on the other is a row of shops and restaurants. I manoeuvre myself out of the car and follow him as he walks along the road to one of the few buildings with lights on. It's a restaurant, its front painted a rich terracotta colour. An awning and a few tables sit outside but they're all unoccupied, and a soft light glows from the windows.

'After you.' George pulls the door open for me. I step inside and am hit by a warm spicy smell. The restaurant is small and cosy, with low lighting against walls of exposed brickwork. Most of the seating is booths, the high-backed seating cushioned in dark blue velvet, on either side of polished dark wooden tables fixed to the walls. A young couple in sportswear huddle together in the booth closest to the back, and an elderly man in a shirt and brown cord trousers is sitting at a small table by the window, leafing through a newspaper.

A tired but smiling man greets us casually. He's wearing a teal shirt and black trousers, and his long hair is woven into thick black braids and tied back against the nape of his neck. He looks at George with familiarity, and then at me with surprise which he quickly conceals.

'Can you squeeze us in?' George says, looking around at the almost empty restaurant.

'I'm sure we can find room for you George.' The man has the accent of a Londoner with Nigerian-born parents.

'Great, thanks Femi.' George gestures to me. 'This is Frannie's best friend Hydie.'

The man lifts his hand in a wave.

'Nice to meet you. Take a seat anywhere, I'll be with you in a moment.' George looks at me as the man walks away.

'Anywhere take your fancy?' I scan the room and nod to the

booth closest to the window. We take seats opposite one another and Femi comes over with two glasses of water and menus printed on thick paper.

'If you have any questions about the menu just ask,' he says, smiling at me, 'don't ask this guy. He pretends he knows about Nigerian food and I catch him googling the dishes under the table.'

'Very cultured,' I say to George, as Femi walks away. He shrugs.

'I'm ignorant, but I know good food when I have it, and everything here is amazing. I could close my eyes and point at the menu and I would love whatever turned up.'

'I've been to a tasting night with Adam and Jay, I recognise some of these dishes.' I scan the menu, picking out things I know I like and, when Femi comes back over, I order the roasted plantain.

'And do you want to share jollof rice?' I ask George. 'Kind of goes with everything.'

'Sounds good,' he says, 'I just need to decide what I want.'

'Why don't you put your money where your mouth is?' I say. 'Close your eyes and point, you know you'll love it, so give yourself the element of surprise.'

'That's not a bad idea,' he says, 'Femi, I want whatever I point to.' Femi raises his eyebrows, but silently puts his pen to his notepad.

George closes his eyes and lifts his hand, casting his index finger above the paper like he's scrying. As he does so I silently reach over and place my fingers on the menu, and, when he lowers his hand, slide the paper carefully along the table until his finger hits pepper soup with scotch bonnets. The spiciest thing on the menu. Femi snorts and quickly lifts his hand to his mouth.

'What?' George says with his eyes still closed, 'What did I

pick?'

'Chicken, fish or goat sir?' Femi says, giving me a sly smile.

'Fish. Unless fish is a bad choice?' George opens his eyes and I whip the menu away before he can see where he'd pointed.

'Coming right up sir.' Femi writes on his notepad with a flourish. 'And I'll get you both some more water for the table.' We exchange a look and he leaves.

'Oh no.' George says. 'What have I done?'

'Nothing.' I smile, 'A fine choice.'

'You couldn't have said anything more ominous.' he says, as Femi returns and places a comically large jug of water on the table.

'Do you come here a lot?' I ask.

'I've been a couple of times, but Femi and I know each other anyway. His brother works with Rowena.'

I resist the urge to shift uncomfortably in my seat.

'So she introduced you to this place? That's nice…' I trail off lamely.

'No, she's not a fan of this sort of food.' George said, 'But I got along really well with Femi when I met him at a party so I come here from time to time. Though not often so late.'

'Do you live close?'

'Just up there,' George gestures out of the window to the right, 'about five minutes away.'

'That's good, so you can come here lots.' I was cringing at my inability to say anything interesting. Though impressed with George's apparent willingness to carry the conversation without any help from me, continuing our mutual, unspoken agreement to let the elephant in the room stay sitting in the corner.

'It's great round here for food. There's this place, of course, there's a Korean barbecue restaurant up the road run by an old couple and their kids. The best pasta in London is made two minutes in the other direction at a place where they don't have any inside seating but they have an awning and put chairs out on the pavement. And there's a proper French patisserie just over the road from my flat. You'll have to try it sometime, you will adore it. You think the pastries we had in Spain were nice? The almond croissants they make there are like these soft pillows in a delicate seashell that crumbles as you bite into it.'

'That does sound amazing.'

'What are you doing tomorrow?' he asks, his eyes brightening, 'we could get coffee there. It's not too far when the overground is running, or I'd come and pick you up again.' He raises an eyebrow when he sees me hesitate. 'Or are you busy again?'

I bristle, feeling like he's trapped me here to talk about this. 'You keep interrogating me about this,' I say, keeping my face neutral, 'I don't love it. I want to spend time with you all but I also have the right to say no to things. I'm not actually part of your family.'

He opens his mouth to say something, then seems to think better of it. He thinks for a moment then says, 'You're right. I'm sorry.' To my surprise he looks uncomfortable, fiddling with his sleeve in a way that is completely unlike him.

'I'll come clean. I'm worried it's because of me.'

'What?' I ask, a sudden dropping sensation in my stomach.

'Everything was fine, and then I came to your room that night... my room, I guess. And the next day you left before me or Nisha could say goodbye. Since then you've not been around as much. I know it probably came out of nowhere for you, but I'd been thinking about it since we were in Spain. For me, it felt like it had been a long time coming. And the next day I realised maybe you hadn't felt as strongly as I had. If I moved too soon then I'm really sorry, and if you're uncomfortable around me because of it I completely accept that. But also Frannie and Nisha still want to see you. I don't want you to lose your friendships with them because of me.'

He trails off, and before I can respond, Femi arrives with our food. My mouth waters at the smell as a plate of roasted plantain with onions and peppers and a sweet spicy dressing is placed in front of me, and a large oval dish of tangy orange rice is set down in the middle between us.

'Now for the surprise.' George says, looking apprehensively at what Femi puts down in front of him. The pepper soup, a thin stew in a sunny, harmless-looking yellow, with a spice level that makes my eyes begin to water just from the scent. As I look closer I see the rings of freshly sliced chilli in the mixture, like wide green and red eyes.

'Shit.' George said. 'I really picked this?'

'Maybe the universe is punishing you for making me talk about awkward subjects in public.'

'I'll take this punishment I suppose,' he said. 'It could have been worse. Do people still get struck by lightning?'

I tuck into my delicious, fragrant food, while George tentatively dips his spoon into his stew.

'If you're hesitant about it it'll be worse,' Femi says, bringing over a sharing spoon for the rice. 'It's like cold water, you just have to dive in.'

George sets his face in a look of grim determination, takes a deep breath, and scoops an enormous spoonful into his mouth. Femi and I both watch as George chews thoughtfully, then swallows.

'Verdict?' I ask softly.

'Holy shit.'

George's eyes go glassy as they begin to water and colour rises in his cheeks, the pink dusky against his skin.

'I'm just going to need to go for it. Don't watch me, it won't be pretty.'

We eat in silence, except for George taking lungfuls of air and gulps of water between mouthfuls, and the soft sniggering that Femi and I exchange every time he walks past, which is more often than any waiter reasonably would.

The restaurant is so warm and comfortable that I'd forgotten it was so late, until George lifts the almost empty bowl to his lips and drinks the last of the spicy soup. He sets down his empty bowl with a look of triumph, as though he's been through some mighty ordeal. I put on a supremely calm and measured display as I take another spoonful of rice, itself well-spiced, and scoop the last of the sliced onion and plantain onto it and lift it into my mouth.

'That was delicious,' I said, 'just the right level of heat. How was yours?'

George takes a napkin and dabs at his wet eyes. 'Mine was alright. Bit bland, they could have spiced it up a bit.'

Femi comes to collect our plates and shakes his head as he passes George a fresh napkin.

'When I first met him,' he says to me, 'this boy here kept talking about his Indian grandparents and their cooking, trying to find common ground. Now look at him.'

'Absolutely humiliating.' George laughs, between taking sharp breaths to draw cold air into his mouth. 'I need some fresh air. How about we pay up and I take you back to yours?' He pays on the card machine that Femi brings him and then, as I'm walking towards the door, I see him pull some notes from his wallet and leave them on the table. The night is dark blue above the lights of London. I think about how clear the stars are in Mijas, where

here the artificial light drowns them out. I check the time on my phone as George joins me.

'The underground is still going. I don't mind getting myself home.'

'Absolutely not,' George said, 'I'll drop you back. I just have one request first.'

'Right?'

'I feel like I'm walking away from Femi with my head held high. Would you agree?'

I nod as he continues. 'I finished my plate, I drank water like a normal person, and I neither cried nor threw up.'

'Your eyes watered a lot.'

'That's just cruel biology,' he says, 'We can look past that. However, I need to go back to my place and drink an entire pitcher of water and maybe stick my head in the freezer.' He looks at his watch. 'We can still be back at yours in an hour, is that okay?'

I nod. 'It's going to be a bad night's sleep whatever happens.'

CHAPTER FOURTEEN

We return to George's car and drive a short distance, through a few streets and into a car park at the base of a large apartment block that opens when George types a code into a keypad at the gate. We walk through the dimly lit car park to a lift that takes us up to the fifth floor. I can feel my heart beating fast as we approach George's apartment. The last time I had seen him we had slept together, and now we were not only alone together, but about to be alone together in the most intimate space possible - his home. He unlocks the door and holds it open for me to walk through, then follows me in and closes it behind him. His apartment is large and clean, while still seeming cosy. He leads me to the living room which has broad white walls, a dark wooden floor, and French windows leading to a small balcony that I can just about make out in the dark. He has a brown leather sofa and a glass coffee table on a woven rug in deep Autumn colours. Beside the couch is a low wooden side table, on which is an enormous, vibrantly green fern plant, sprouting from a tall vase painted in a blue and white herringbone pattern. On the biggest wall is a shelving unit crammed with books and records, the top of which is decorated with a smattering of photos in glass frames of his family and friends. I recognise, with a flutter of delight, the photo taken of Frannie, Nisha, Lila and I during the photoshoot in Mijas.

'I like your fern,' I say.

'It's nice isn't it?' George says, 'I'm not sure I could keep a pet flourishing at this time in my life, but this guy is doing well. Now, excuse me while I drown myself in ice water.'

He leaves to go through another door. I hear the opening of kitchen cupboards and the running of a tap. When he returns his face is damp, the curls that frame his face darkened and shiny. He's holding a soft white towel in one hand and a fresh glass of water in the other which he offers to me. We stand on the rug facing one another.

'Femi's right you know,' he says, pressing the towel into his face once I've taken the glass from him. 'My sisters can both handle spice much better than I can. But I also don't think traditional Indian food has as much heat as people think. I think a lot of the spicier stuff people have here was made for restaurants. The food my grandparents make is fragrant and rich, but I don't think it ever hurts to eat it.'

'Do you feel okay now?'

'I'm fine. I'm a big boy.'

I feel a twinge of guilt at his flushed cheeks, and I have to confess.

'It's my fault,' I say, folding my arms against myself. 'I moved the menu when you had your eyes closed. I made you pick pepper soup. I was trying to be funny but it was probably quite mean. I didn't realise it would be that spicy.'

To my surprise, George smiles. 'Okay well, then we've both got a confession to make.' He looks around as though someone could be listening in, then leans towards me. 'I know you moved the menu because I had my eyes open.'

'Oh god, you already knew.' I put my face in my hands, cringing at myself.

'Hydie, stop.' George reaches out and gently pulls my fingers away from my eyes, holding them as though if he lets go I'll cover my face again. 'I like the pepper soup and I like spicy food just fine. If I didn't want it I would have just ordered something else. You didn't do anything wrong, you were just playing. You have to stop feeling so guilty about things.'

'I was already feeling guilty about missing the barbecue.' I say, ruffled.

'I'm sorry I hassled you about it.'

'It's okay. You're right I've not been a very good friend lately.'

'Neither have I.' He's still holding my fingertips in his hands. All I want in that moment is to ask him if he remembers what I told him when I was younger, to ask if that still shapes how he sees me. Because it's never felt more important that I know these things as George steps closer and I tilt my head to meet his lips.

George is tentative at first, his mouth parting in a barely there kiss as he waits for my reaction then, when I press my mouth against his, he drops my hands and slides his arms around my waist pulling me close. I slide my fingers up his arms to lace against the back of his neck, feeling the soft curls at the base of his skull. I gently push my hands upwards and into his hair. Need shimmers in my body as I feel his hands tighten around my waist. He grips me hard, and the slight pain makes me gasp, just enough for him to press his tongue into my open mouth. I taste the lingering spice, the flavour gone, but the sharp sting remaining. He could lift me if he wanted to, I realise. He could do anything to me if he wanted to. I become aware of the way his hands are moving gently across my back, his fingers feeling out the buttons on the back of my dress. Unsure of how best to tell him what I want, and unwilling to break the kiss to use words, I drop my hand to his waist behind his back and slide the tips of my fingers just beneath his belt.

He hisses through his teeth and makes a low guttural noise that resonates in my bones, as though it is activating something ancient in me. I pull away slightly, freeing my mouth to ask if we can go to his bedroom, and look into his face, his dark eyes more fiery than I've ever seen them, his usually sweet, smiling face is intense. I decide I can't wait, I can't take my eyes away from him. Instead, I take his shirt roughly in my two fists and, smiling at my own assertiveness, pull him firmly towards his couch. I drop myself down and, before he can crash down into me, pull his belt off. He puts a hand out to graze the top of my head as I undo the buttons of his jeans and pull them down with his underwear to reveal his hardening cock beneath.

'Oh fuck.' George says, almost to himself, as I open my mouth and take the whole length in. He hardens completely in an instant, and as I move my head back and forth I feel him grow too big for my mouth. I put a hand up at the base of his dick to steady myself and take it firmly, feeling the tip against the back of my throat. George's knees buckle slightly and as I slide him out of my mouth, dragging my tongue beneath his length I see him plant a hand flat against the wall behind the couch, his eyes shut tight in that way people do, where intense pleasure looks like pain. I find myself smiling round his cock as I take him in again and feel his breathing deepen as I fall into a steady rhythm, sucking him hard and fast, beads of salty precum finding their way to my tongue. As his heavy breathing turns to moans I speed up, surprised at myself. I want him to finish in my mouth, to find out what he tastes like.

As I get faster and faster his eyes open and, with a look so intense he almost looks angry, he pushes off against the wall and takes me roughly by the shoulders, pulling me away from him. I make an involuntary mewling sound as my mouth is suddenly empty, but he moves me roughly around and places me on all fours on the couch, pulling my dress up above my waist and pulling my underwear down until they sit around my thighs.

'Hey Hydie,' I hear him behind me as he kneels behind me, feeling the tip of his cock, thick and hard against my entrance.

'Yeah?' I say, tilting my hips and trying to slide back into him. He stops me with a firm hand on my back.

'Is there any angle I put can you at where you're not unbelievably fuckable?'

I begin to reply, to cheekily suggest we try some, but he pushes roughly inside me and the words melt into a cry of pleasure. I'm shunted forward by the movement and bury my head in the couch, the leather warm and soft against my face as George holds my hips and fucks me. The angle lets him push deep inside me, the sensation such intense pleasure that I have to bite my teeth into my lower lip to keep from grunting or screaming. I arch my back more, trying to find a way to take him even deeper, as though I want to feel this in my whole body. My hands are slippy on the couch, and I feel my own wetness against the inside of my thighs. For a bizarre moment, it occurs to me to apologise for the state we'll be leaving his couch, but I couldn't form the words if I tried.

George shifts behind me, leaning forward over my back, his body completely flush against mine, filling me completely, and I feel him slide a hand from my hip down and between my legs, where his fingers touch gently against my clit. The sound I make is undignified, the movement ungainly. I say 'fuck' in a hiss between my teeth and lunge myself back and forth, against his hand and his cock. I hear him make a deep, satisfied sound as he lets me move the way I want, grinding against him. I cum quicker than I want, the intensity building and spilling over, and then I lie in the flooding pleasure, feeling him ride the wave of my orgasm until almost at his own. He pulls out and I feel him shudder as he finishes, spilling hot and wet against the back of my legs.

We stay like that for a few moments, both of us catching our breath. Then I stand and straighten my dress as George does his belt back up again.

'Can I go to the bathroom?' I say, 'Just to sort myself out before I mess up your couch?' I gesture to my legs

George tells me where it is and I follow the corridor round to a bathroom tiled in neat white squares. It's as though I'm splashing my face in a sheet of graph paper. Above the sink is a set of grey men's skincare identical to the set at his parent's house. When I've finished cleaning myself up I walk back through the corridor and pass George going the other way. He gives me a kiss on the cheek as I walk past him and I sit back down on the couch which, miraculously, looks as though nothing at all has happened there. I sit myself neatly on the leather, tucking the skirt of my dress around my legs.

I make myself laugh, sitting so primly on a couch on which I have just been roughly fucked by its owner. I realise I still haven't seen George's bedroom. I wonder what it looks like, whether it has the same warm colours and rich fabrics as the living room. I think about searching for the patisserie George mentioned on my phone, choosing what to have in the morning when we go there together. I wish I'd brought the travel toothbrush from Frannie's house. I wish I'd brought pyjamas, but why would I have? To think just a few hours ago I had been waiting for him at the door, unsure he would even turn up.

The bathroom door opens and closes, and I hear his footsteps approach his shadow on the wall before he comes back around the corner.

'Are you okay?' I say, reflexively as we make eye contact.

'Yeah,' he says, but his tone is unexpectedly strained. He sits down, a person's width away from me on the couch. I go to move across to him. To close the gap, as I do so he catches my wrists, keeping me at a distance, holding them between us awkwardly, as though he's not sure what to do with them.

'Hydie, listen. I'm sorry,' he says, and I feel a dropping sensation in my chest.

'For what?' I try to smile, 'I thought it was pretty good.'

He gives me a weak smile, humouring me, but looks so uncomfortable that I draw back, moving my arms out of his grip, and sit back against the other arm of the couch.

'What's wrong?'

'I just,' he looks away, his expression one of shame. 'You're wonderful and I love spending time with you. But it's not been that long since I ended things with-' He chews his lip. 'I think I've made a mistake.'

'A mistake?'

'I told myself I needed to wait at least until after Frannie's wedding, but I couldn't help myself. I should have been more disciplined. I should have controlled my feelings.'

'You don't have to control anything.' I say. 'I like you and, if I'm reading the signs right, which I assume I am, you like me, what's the problem?'

'It's not right.' He says. 'I'm just out of a relationship. You're Frannie's best friend. You're a lot younger than I am. There's a lot to untangle. We should have talked before anything happened.'

'Maybe things haven't happened in the most ideal circumstances, or in the best timeframe. But now things have happened. We can't undo that, so what do you want?'

'That's the problem though isn't it?' George says. He's looking at his hands in his lap, as though he can't bear to face me. 'All I've been thinking about is what I want. My own feelings. When I should have been thinking about what's best for you.'

'Best for me?' It was bizarre to hear him speak like this.

'I should have made sure you were comfortable.'

'I think me enthusiastically undressing us both was a signal that I was comfortable.'

'Not in the moment. In general.'

'George, what are you talking about?'

'Look, you're very young still. Thirty and twenty-five are two different stages in life. It's not responsible of me to act like this with you. I should be looking out for you, not sleeping with you.'

'You think my age is a problem?' I feel hot, suddenly. The leather of the couch sticks to the skin of my legs. 'I'm not a kid anymore. I'm twenty five not fifteen. You don't need to "look after me". It makes me feel as though you don't think I'm your equal. You don't need to help me like you help everyone else. I don't want to be helped, like I'm something to be pitied, I want to be seen as an adult who can make her own decisions.'

'I didn't mean it that way,' he says.

'Then how did you mean it?'

He doesn't reply and we sit in a silence that I don't know how to fill. I'm not going to plead like some lovesick puppy, and I'm also too bewildered to argue with him, or even to cover my feelings and make a joke to ease the tension.

Instead, I sit on the couch while George tells me that I'm still his guest, and that I should stay the night, that he'll give me a lift home in the morning. His politeness is excruciating. His tone is that of a polite neighbour offering to lend me a lawnmower. He offers to stay on the couch while I sleep in his bed, but I gather the presence of mind to insist that I be the one sleeping in the living room. The idea of going into his bedroom and lying there without him is completely sickening.

'Probably for the best,' he tries to joke as he pulls a pillow and blankets out of a cupboard in the hall. 'I haven't hoovered in a couple of days and there's a pile of laundry you could fall into and get lost.'

I don't laugh, and there is a prolonged and nightmarish silence as he makes up a bed for me.

'If you need anything else let me know,' he says with a forced, friendly tone. He's trying so hard to act normal that he's doing everything as though being held at gunpoint. And I stand there, humiliated, utterly unwilling to lower the weapon.

After a few awkward minutes he bids me goodnight and tells me that he'll drop me back home at about half past eight. He doesn't offer to take me to the patisserie beforehand. He gives a strange little wave as he closes his bedroom door and I return it with a grim smile.

And then he leaves me there, standing by the couch on which I have just had incredible sex, and the most painfully bizarre conversation. Whatever liquid delight I had been feeling earlier in the evening has cooled to stiff marble. I sit in the dark on the couch, not touching the blanket or pillows he's laid out. I stare grimly at the fern plant in its pot, resisting the urge to knock it over. I map out this part of London as best I can in my head, remembering which underground lines close at night. Then I pick up my things and leave the apartment, closing the door gently so George doesn't hear, and take the stairs down to the street to catch a convoluted selection of tube lines home.

CHAPTER FIFTEEN

Adam and Jay look up from their lunch when I emerge into the kitchen the next morning. I had gotten home and curled up fully dressed in bed, not waking until past noon. Even Millie looks surprised, padding towards me like an accusing parent.

'Good morning. Well, good afternoon.' Adam smiles slyly as Jay gets up silently to make me a coffee. 'Glad you're back. Where were you sneaking off to in the wee small hours last night?'

'I'm sorry I didn't message you guys. I hope you weren't worried?'

'We were a bit confused, but we thought we'd wait until you didn't come home before we rounded up a search party.'

'Is everything okay?' Jay asks, pouring me a glass of water from the pitcher on the table.

They haven't asked me where I was or what I was doing, which I appreciate. But in this moment I feel too full of what's just happened, and need to share it with someone.

'I was with George, Frannie's brother.'

'Oh,' Adam says, and I can feel his restraint as he stops himself asking anything. Jay pulls a chair out for me and sits back down to his breakfast. I join them, pleased to be sat in the warm, with people who make me comfortable, after a night with so much strangeness. I tell them what happened.

Predictably, Jay listens with an impassive expression, occasionally making sympathetic noises, while Adam remains completely silent as his face goes through every expression possible.

'Well, well, well,' he finally says as I lay out my journey home through a tangle of late night underground services. 'A late-night rendezvous with your best friend's, much older, only-just-single brother. Who would have known you had that in you?'

'How do you feel?' Jay asks. I make a noncommittal noise.

'Right now I just feel tired. But I think when I've had some sleep I'll be either embarrassed or annoyed, or possibly both.'

'Why would *you* be embarrassed? It sounds like he's the one acting like an idiot.'

'Because,' I hesitate, deciding how much to say. 'Because I've liked him since I was a teenager. I know that's a bit weird, but after meeting him again as an adult I realised that I still feel the same way. When I was with him this evening I thought it meant that he finally saw us as being past the point where age gaps matter. And then he made me feel like I can never outgrow the kid he knew.'

'I can have sympathy for him.' Jay says thoughtfully. 'He clearly likes you, but you are younger than him, and there are things that you both need to consider. Is he over his breakup? How would Frannie feel if she found out? He's right that jumping into bed - or on a sofa - was too quick, and he's the one with the ex and the sister. He's the one who should be responsible for considering them.'

'Oh Jay, you're being too nice,' Adam rolls his eyes at me. 'This guy seems like a complete stick to me, Hydie. It's like he's so desperate to do the right thing all the time that he ends up causing problems in the process. It's the classic paradox of the people pleaser.'

'So you think leaping into bed with Hydie and giving her all sorts of ideas, even if you're unable to commit to anything further, was the right move?'

'Hydie's a grown woman, not some sad abandoned puppy. He might have hurt her in the end, but this way he's hurting her anyway. He clearly likes her but he's messed up anything between them without even giving them a chance.'

They're talking about me as though I'm not there, trading opinions until Adam makes a snide joke about foiled book jackets and they completely leave the topic. I sit silently at the table, my head heavy with tiredness.

They're both right, in a way. George initiated everything that had happened between us, then pushed me away. That had been a bad thing to do. But perhaps he truly thought it was for the best. Perhaps he was thinking of my friendship with Frannie, as well as my friendship with both Nisha and himself. If George and I entered into a messy situationship that ended on bad terms, the awful awkwardness caused could have been completely unsalvageable.

And yet even while I think all of this, a horrible alternative occurs to me. George himself said that it was too soon after his breakup, but he had initiated everything. Perhaps he had just been using me. Perhaps he had just needed something to get past his breakup, and I happened to have been there and willing. It wasn't the George I knew, but as I thought about it I realised that perhaps I was thinking of a George that existed ten years ago. Transplanting that boy onto a man who had become completely different.

I don't know which was true. And in the end, it doesn't really matter. Either way, I feel bruised and furious. That George could allow me to taste something I had wanted for so long and then push me away again had felt so painful that I couldn't stand it, and to still not know if George felt the same way I did is dizzying to the point of nausea.

Something touches my hand, which is resting on my lap beneath the table. It is Millie's nose, and I lift my hand to stroke her soft ears as she rests her head on my knee. Adam and Jay's discussion has faded to background noise and, without saying anything, I get up and leave the table. Millie, as if knowing I need comfort, follows me up the stairs to my room and sits hopefully next to my bed as I change into pyjamas and get under the duvet. When I pat the space next to me she jumps up to fill it. I fall asleep comforted by her soft warmth, and the gentle rise and fall of her breathing.

*

I wake up a few hours later and, once I've established in a panic that I'm not supposed to be at work, type out a message to Frannie. I tell her that I'm sorry I've missed a few things, that I've been busy and feeling a bit under the weather, and ask if she would like to catch up for coffee soon, just us two. As I brush my teeth and wash off the makeup I reflect on the bizarre events of the last night. For a while, I wonder if George is reflecting in the same way, but decide that it shouldn't matter to me anymore.

As I replay the scene in my head, I feel once again the sharp sting of rejection. I realise that I'm not only remembering the pain of the night before, but that of another night as well. As though connected through ten years I remember the way George had let go of my hands, so much smaller than his back then, the same pitying expression, and realise that all I have done, after everything, is repeated the same experience, baring my soul only to have it crushed to pulp in the name of doing the right thing

With grim determination I mentally write off the possibility of anything happening between me and George. As strong as my feelings have been for him, I conclude that, ultimately, the events of last night ended the way they needed to for me. Whatever George's intentions, his actions closed a door in my head that I had allowed to linger open for too long. I had pushed away other elements of my past, and if I was going to have a relationship with Frannie that wasn't being constantly overshadowed by my childish crush on her brother, George would just have to be consigned to the same emotional graveyard. I would see him if I had to, I would be civil and friendly, but I wouldn't indulge in the friendship, forcing it to bear a meaning and significance that only I was giving it.

I would put my focus where it belonged, in my friendship with Frannie, whose love I knew was unconditional, and exactly as I needed it to be. I would work to create a friendship with Frannie which did not need me to see George more than necessary. I knew I would have to see him at the wedding. I would not hide, nor would I pretend nothing had happened. I wasn't avoiding him anymore. Instead I would get through it with as much dignity as I could, then leave George where he belonged, in the daydreams and letters and star-shaped box of a stupid little girl.

Ten Years Ago

When the Star Girlz track began, every girl in the venue cried out in joy. In the crush of bodies, Frannie grabbed me, the glitter around her eyes sparkling in the light like a galaxy.

'Was this you?' she squealed with delight. 'Was this your idea?'

'It was George's idea!' I laughed 'I just helped choose the songs.'

Over the crowd I could see him laughing with delight, the other adult attendees at the party looking on as twenty teenage girls flung themselves at one another, screaming the lyrics as the song started up.

'Why don't you meet me at midnight baby!' We all shouted at the ceiling of the venue, spangled with spinning lights. 'Why can't you see how much I-I-I want you to see me!' The song was lush with yearning and desire, and as I jumped up and down with the rest of the girls I saw George smiling at us, smiling, I fantasised, directly at me, revelling in our shared victory as much as I had.

Until the first Star Girlz track had come on, Frannie's party guests had been standing in small groups, chatting and singing along to the music. The plan had been to affectionately embarrass Frannie, but instead the song had lifted the party to a place of shared joy. Girls who had never met before were jumping into each other's arms and holding hands, their emotions renewed each time the next song started and they once again heard the beginning of a song they had loved as a child, discovering that they still knew it by heart.

When the music eventually faded and the party drifted towards its end, Frannie grabbed my hand and pulled me off the dancefloor. We stumbled towards the table of food and both drank deeply from the large plastic cups of water. I felt flushed and dizzy, had screamed and smiled more than I thought I ever had in my life, carried away in the crowd.

'There's the birthday girl.' George said, approaching us at the table. 'Hello trouble,' he looked directly at me, 'I wondered if we'd lose you both in that tangle of happy Star Girlz fans.'

Without warning Frannie pulled both of us towards her, embracing us both at the same time.

'Thank you,' she said 'I can't believe you did that for me. I had forgotten all about those songs.' The shaking of her shoulders told me she was crying, her face pressed against George's chest.

'I'm happy you're so happy, Frannie,' he laughed, 'We thought it would be a little prank but it turned out to be so much better.' George put his arms around his sister and, by default, me. I tried not to tremble as I felt myself pressed into him. He planted a soft kiss on the top of his sister's head, and smiled at me, before gently untangling himself from us and walking away. I watched him go, my heart ringing like a bell, as Frannie continued to talk to me, watching him slip out of the back door of the hall, where the pool was, where we had all played volleyball earlier in the day.

'Why don't we just take it?' Frannie was saying when I returned my attention to her. She was holding a large bottle of Prosecco, from which all the girls had had tiny glasses poured and handed out by Frannie's parents. I hadn't enjoyed it, sharp and sour, but Frannie took the bottle by the neck and led me out of a side door to sit on the steps in the dying light.

We each took a drink straight from the bottle, and she rested her head on my shoulder.

'I wish you were my sister,' she said, her voice a little clumsier than usual.

'I wish I was too,' I felt her giggle against my shoulder.

'Maybe you should marry George,' she said mischievously. I laughed, trying to sound normal, as though her words hadn't shot me full of nerves. I took another drink from the bottle. With each sip the sour taste was transformed into something deep and sophisticated, like I was swallowing starlight.

'Or maybe we need to marry two brothers,' she said, 'maybe if we found twins we both liked.'

'What if we got them mixed up one day?' I said. Frannie burst into laughter.

'Well, I'm sure they would tell us.'

We sat together on the little step of the doorway for a while longer, feeling the effects of the alcohol moving through us. I had never been even tipsy before, I felt as though I were in an old film, everything just slightly blurred and given a warm, hazy tone. We heard Frannie's mother calling for her and she got to her feet, slightly wobbly in her strappy heels. I got up after her, my hands out to steady her. My own body was stable, though my mind felt strange, as though my thoughts were underwater. She passed me, to go in through the door to find her parents.

'Are you coming?' she asked. I felt hot. Autumn was unseasonably warm, and the time in the sun earlier in the day had burned my shoulders, and the cooler evening wind felt soothing against them, against my cheeks and chapped lips.

'I'll be another minute.' I said and turned away. I walked carefully around the walls of the house, thinking only of the coolness against my skin until I saw blue lights dancing against the wall, walking towards them as though drawn to will-o'-the-wisps in a forest. As I turned the corner I realised I had been seeing the lights on the outside of the venue, bouncing off the water in the pool, which was still lit and uncovered, casting a blue shimmer across the little courtyard like a mermaid's lagoon. As I approached I heard him.

'Hello, trouble. Fancy seeing you here.'

I jumped, caught off guard, alone with him. He was leaning against the wooden fencing that divided the house from the rest of the world. Behind him, a thin moon was glowing silver, like a coin caught mid-flip. He smiled at me in the dark, and I could feel my love-struck heart thudding against my chest.

'Thank you for your help with today,' he said. 'I really appreciate it. Frannie loves you so much, and it made her birthday perfect.'

I was fizzing with the excitement of the party, of the warmth of the sun earlier in the day that had sunk into my skin. Prosecco sparkled in my stomach. I was giddy with feelings, the carefully held emotions I had for him were spilling through my hands and

I felt as though I had to give them to him, as though the sheer power of the feelings I had for him meant that he must surely feel them for me too.

He watched me, his eyes questioning as I stepped towards him, my hands twisting nervously, but my mind bold and sure. I opened my mouth.

I have spent ten years trying to pretend that night didn't happen. If I think back on that moment I see it as if watching the scene from the side. I see myself small and pale in front of him, a child gazing at him as though I were approaching some mythical being. From where I stand in my mind, watching a child approach someone who is so much older than she is, it is so obviously wrong. After I had told him how I felt there had been the most awful silence, like the moment after a gunshot, and in that second I had come to my senses, realised what I had done. I remember feeling as though I was crumpling to the ground, even though my body wouldn't move. I wanted to run away and hide, I wanted to disappear into mist. But I stayed, looking at him in horror.

He had walked towards me, and taken my hand in his and for a moment I had thought he was going to kiss me. Even now I remember the sudden terror, feeling how small my fingers had been as his had closed round them.

'I am so flattered,' he said carefully, 'that someone as wonderful as you would feel that way about me. And when you feel this way about someone your own age they will be incredibly lucky.'

And I had said nothing. He had put his hand gently on the top of my head and walked back into the house, leaving me staring at the moon, a mocking white smile that had watched the whole thing.

A few minutes later I had come back into the house and,

avoiding George, had found Frannie's father and told him I was feeling unwell. I had looked so pale and distressed he hadn't asked any questions, just beckoned Frannie over to say goodnight before taking me to his car and driving me back to my home. I remember it was the only time he had spoken to my mother, thought it strange at the time, though now I know he must have been worried I wouldn't be properly looked after. He had touched the top of my head in the same way George had before he left, which had opened the wound anew and I had run past my mother to my room and howled silently into my pillow.

For a decade, I had tried to push down the pain of that night. It had cost me my relationship with Frannie's family, it had almost cost me my relationship with Frannie herself. And yet, it had always been there. However much I ignored it. Curled in my chest, like a little animal. I felt it now, sitting on my bed as I thought about his hands on my skin, the thrill of his mouth on mine. Everything was falling in on itself, and I was somehow both people at once, the two rejections finding each other through time and fusing to create something all-consuming, like a collapsing star.

CHAPTER SIXTEEN

I see the text from George that night on my phone an hour before I answer it. Once I've read it I put my phone down and have a bath, using a bubble mix that I have been saving since Christmas, deciding that I deserve a 'Lavender Sugar Cookie' scented treat. I put together a salad lunch of green beans and fresh pasta, tossed with feta, lemon and walnuts and eat with Jay and Adam, who studiously avoid asking how I am. Then I sit on the sofa in my pyjamas and open my messages.

Hey, just dropping a message to say I'm so sorry for last night. If there's any way I can make it up to you let me know xx

I had been expecting the text. Could have predicted the wording even. And so I reply, having decided what I would say hours beforehand.

Hi. It's all good, don't worry about it. See you at the wedding if I don't before x

And then I turn my attention away. Frannie has replied to my message, so we arrange to meet for dinner after work later in the week. When that evening comes around I finish up at the stationery shop and take the overground to the apartment building where Frannie lives with Theo.

When I get there Frannie buzzes me into the building and I take the lift up and follow the corridor round as per her instructions.

She opens the door before I knock and pulls me in for a hug. I hug her back and she leads me into her home. I'd visited her flat a few times before, but she's redecorated since. The walls of her living room are cream, with a dark green couch and several vases of flowers on the coffee table, windowsill and cabinets. I find myself looking at a tall clay vase with fresh peonies in it. For a moment I can't tell why it's caught my attention, but then realise with a jolt that it's the same vase that George had beside his couch. The blue and white vase filled with the fern plant.

'It's nice isn't it?' Frannie says, in an uncanny echo of George. 'Our aunt Patricia, you met her in Mijas, bought matching ones for me and the siblings. It was sort of a joke about how we would always fight as children if she bought us different presents, but actually, they suit all of our homes even though we put different things in them.'

'What does Nisha put in hers?' I ask.

'She loves baby's breath. I think the last time I went to her place she had a bouquet of it with gladioli and statice. She likes flowers that look like they're spraying into the air. I like a more solid, chunky look.' She reaches out and gently pets the tops of the pink peonies as though they are little pets. 'And I think George has some big green leafy things. Ferns? Something manly.'

I change the subject. 'Does Theo want any help in the kitchen?'

'He'll be fine.' Frannie says, 'We'll say hello then leave him to it. I've got a surprise for you.'

I follow her into the spacious kitchen where Theo is peeling the rind from a lemon into neat curls next to a pot of bubbling pasta sheets.

'Hey Hydie.' he says to me without looking up.

'You're so good at that.' Frannie says. 'I always get that bitter pith underneath.' She opens a cupboard door and reaches to the top shelf, pulling down three highball glasses.

'It's a school night and Theo needs to be up early, so we can't go crazy.' She says placing them on the counter and retrieving a tray of ice from the freezer. 'But I was thinking we could do mocktails.'

She mixes lemon juice, cucumber water and seltzer, pouring it over ice and garnishing with the rinds of lemon peel that Theo has coiled into thin, bright spirals.

When we have our drinks I follow Frannie up her stairs, treading softly on her pale grey carpet, walking across her landing to the room she shares with Theo. I almost laugh at how perfectly Frannie it is. The walls are a pale lilac, the bedding deep violet, the wardrobe and bedside tables minimal and Venetian, matching a huge vanity with a mirror and wingbacked chair, scattered with nail polish bottles, skincare and perfume. The whole room sparkles.

'What?' she asks, clearly reading my expression as I cast my eyes around.

'Does Theo sleep here too or…?'

'Oh, don't,' she rolls her eyes, 'He has a study where he works which is full of sports memorabilia, and a gaming room which is a shrine to every film and TV franchise he cares about. Trust me he's all good. I'm the one who needs to keep one room as a sanctuary.'

She takes my drink and puts both glasses down on coasters on the bedside table.

'This is why I brought you up here.' She opens the wardrobe and reaches for a zip-up suit bag. 'I was going to bring it to Nisha's barbecue but this will do. I need you to try this on.'

I stifle a gasp as she opens the bag and carefully pulls out a bridesmaid dress. It's a soft, pale seafoam green, a wrap dress in a satin material that catches the light as Frannie holds it by the hanger and turns it around for me.

'What do you think?' she asks. 'I think it will really suit you.'

'It's perfect.' I reach out to touch my fingertips to the fabric, cautiously, as though worried I'll stain it.

'Try it on,' Frannie says, holding out the hanger for me to take from her. 'I just need to know if we need a different size or if it needs to be altered.'

Frannie drapes it across my outstretched arms and I carry the dress like a princess to her bathroom. Gently and carefully I take off the jeans and top I arrived in and step into the dress. Frannie's bathroom mirror only shows my head and shoulders, and I stare at my reflection, wishing I had done my hair, the blonde waves messy against the beautiful fabric and the delicate neckline.

Frannie makes a high-pitched noise, very unlike her, as I step out of the bathroom.

'Look at you Hydie, you look gorgeous.' She jumps up and turns her full-length mirror towards me. Frannie has always had exquisite taste, and the dress is no exception. I can feel the high quality of the fabric, of the cut and stitching, from the way it sits so neatly against my body. The colour brings out the cool, blush tones of my skin, making me look brighter and fresher. The simple sweetheart neckline and short floaty sleeves frame the top of my figure, while the skirt expands into light Grecian pleating that grazes my shins. Frannie gets up and pulls my hair off my shoulders and lifts it into a coil at the nape of my neck.

'I'm thinking with your hair like this,' she says, taking a finger and looping a thin strand of hair from my forehead out so it drifts down into a single curl. 'I think you'll look perfect.'

For a brief moment, my treacherous mind wonders what George would think if he saw me, what he *will* think when he sees me. The thought is unwelcome, a match lighting in a cluttered room, and I snuff it out before anything else catches light. It is not important what my friend's brother thinks about me. It is important that Frannie is happy with how I will look at her wedding. I repeat these two sentences in my head like a mantra as Frannie turns me round checking that the dress fits. She concludes that it fits perfectly, but that the skirt needs to be two inches shorter. I stand still as she slides a tiny safety pin into the inner stitching of the dress where it needs to be cut.

Afterwards, I change again, not wanting to stay in the dress in case anything damages the delicate fabric. Frannie shows me what she'll be wearing before and after the wedding. Her Abuela's dress is gorgeous but heavy and ornate, so outside of the chapel Frannie will be wearing a beautiful silken trouser suit in a deep plum colour. She zips both back into fabric bags and tucks them back into her wardrobe. She sits in her vanity chair while I sit on her bed. I can smell Theo's cooking downstairs.

'I meant to ask,' she says, twirling a coil of lemon peel in her glass 'We now have room for a plus one if you want to bring anyone. I realised I never even asked you, which was rude of me. You've never mentioned anybody, but when you can't come to things I sometimes wonder if you've just got other - obligations.' She puts a stress on the word. She's pretending to be joking but I can tell she's been dying to ask me for weeks.

'I don't need a plus one,' I say immediately. Frannie's face falls. I hesitate, wondering if I should tell her anything. In the end I decide on a version of the truth.

'I thought there was someone for a while,' I say 'We met through mutual friends and I liked him. I thought he liked me back, but I think I was wrong. I don't think he feels the same way.'

Despite my attempts to seem casual as I speak, my words catch in my throat slightly and I feel, with horror, the sting of tears at the corners of my eyes. I quickly take a drink hoping Frannie hasn't noticed. But when I put it down she stands up from the bed and takes my hands in hers.

'Well he's a fool,' she says, 'and if you want to be set up with an endless line of cute boys who would go head over heels for a bookish little blonde in a cardigan just say the word, I definitely know one guy at least.'

'Maybe another time,' I laugh 'but for now, safe to say I don't need a plus one to your party. Maybe Lila can invite that boy she likes.'

Frannie laughs, 'Camilo? Maybe. Though I think she'd prefer to invite Paloma the cat.'

Theo calls from downstairs. The smell of the dinner is glorious and we return to the kitchen to find the dining table set for three, and a large oven dish of bubbling lasagne in the middle. As we seat ourselves at the table a thought occurs to me.

'Why do you suddenly have an extra plus one?'

Frannie gasps and Theo says 'Frannie have you not told her?'

Frannie puts her hands out in front of her, as though preparing me for life-changing news.

'Rowena,' she says slowly, 'is officially out of the picture.'

'It's the scandal of the century.' Theo says, dishing up lasagne onto our plates while Frannie continues.

'And get this Hydie. They've been broken up for months. Months! And George didn't tell us. Why would he not tell us that he'd finally ended things with someone so completely obviously wrong for him? Why wouldn't he tell us he'd finally turned his brain back on?'

'Why indeed?' Theo mutters. I catch his eye and smirk.

Between us we tactfully change the subject, bringing Frannie's attention back to wedding plans. It's all falling into place, she tells me, the food, the flowers, the guests. I nod along silently, occasionally interjecting to say that something sounds lovely, or that a quirk they've decided on is a good idea. It all sounds so involved. Long strings of emails and phone calls, endless negotiating and adjusting. And yet Frannie thrives on it all. So does Theo, I realise, who is enthusiastically joining in with his own laundry list of objectives that have been ticked off. As I watch them I realise that they trade back and forth between being the admirer and the admired, praising one another's hard work and always pointing out to me if the other is underselling some part they played in creating the perfect day for themselves.

I've never had a partner that came close to someone I felt as though I wanted to marry. I had boyfriends here and there, mostly good men, relationships that ended because we weren't quite right for one another. I never thought much about a wedding day because I had never felt it was right to have such concrete ideas about what you want before you know who you want it with.

It occurs to me, as I listen to Theo and Frannie talk, that perhaps part of the point of planning a wedding, a big elaborate day when two people could visit a registry office and have done with it, was the intense planning. A lifetime's worth of admin, logistics and compromise, compressed into a matter of months, which served as a baptism of fire for the experience of married life. And I feel as I sit with them, Theo serving seconds of lasagne while Frannie pours another round of mocktails, that they would do just fine.

But I also feel lonely. The realisation creeps up on me as I watch the tender fondness they have for each other. I have never observed their relationship so close up before. Any couple can post photos of staged love, or write earnest captions on social media. But the way Frannie's fingertips linger against the back of Theo's hand as she puts his drink down on the table, the tiny smile they exchange when they speak, visible only for a moment. It isn't a show. It isn't put on for me, to either impress or exclude me. It's part of the fabric of their relationship. An intimate language made of tiny gestures that convey over and over again, 'I love you'. It's not something I have ever really identified in any of my relationships, the last of which had lasted only four months, over two years ago. And I feel very bereft all of a sudden.

When George and had connected again, when he had come to me in his bedroom, I had felt as though maybe the absence of meaningful relationships in my life had been because he had been the right one all along. Though I hadn't consciously realised it, I had hoped that the fifteen-year-old I had been, had met the right man for her, just ten years earlier than she should have. But I had been wrong. I was on my own. A lone bird in a nature documentary, endlessly calling into the void while all around it others pair and make their nests.

After dinner, I say goodnight to Theo at their front door, as Frannie puts on her shoes to walk me to the bottom of the flat.

'See you soon.' He gives me a big hug. 'We're so happy you'll be there with us.'

'I'm happy too.' I smile at him. I'm not lying. I'm holding my loneliness in one hand, and holding my love for them in the other. I contain multitudes.

Frannie walks me down to the glass doors at the front of their apartment block. We hug goodbye and, to my surprise, she kisses the side of my head, her lips pressing briefly against my hair above where it's tucked behind my ear.

'What was that for?' I smile, as we half pull away.

'I just love you,' she says, 'I'm a bit overwhelmed thinking about this wedding, there's so much happening and so much to think about. It's like my mind is waterlogged with it. But then I remember it's just a day. It's just paper. The important thing is that Theo and I will be married, and we get to share the day with all the people we love. And I'm so excited that you'll be there.' To my surprise, I hear her voice hitch slightly, as though heavy with emotion and I put my arms around her again, feeling her jaw resting against my shoulder.

CHAPTER SEVENTEEN

For the weeks leading up to the wedding, I carefully coordinate seeing Frannie without seeing George. For the first time in my life I am proactive, carefully making sure that each time I part from Frannie, we have the next social plan in place.

At first I'm nervous about accepting plans to see Nisha and Lila, or Frannie's parents, but after a while, I realise George must have gotten the memo, and be bowing out of things so that Frannie can see me. After all this time, he's now the one avoiding me. The irony of it isn't lost on me. He was worried he was the reason I'd begun to pull away again, and the night he told me that had made me determined to find a way to be part of Frannie's life without him.

I do miss him though. Over dinner one night Nisha and Frannie begin a long argument about the talents of a reality TV star-turned-actress, and I know, had he been there, George and I would have shot one another a look of fond dismay. Earlier that evening I had sat with Lila at Nisha's kitchen table and asked her about school and, carefully, tried to ask her about the letter she wanted to give to Camilo. She had gone pink and tried to answer vaguely, and I had spared her by quickly changing the subject, asking instead about the notepaper she had found in the stationery shop, and whether she wanted any more.

'I can always bring some over if you like?'

'It's okay, I think I wrote what I wanted to, thank you.' Lila says, 'But maybe I can ask Uncle George to take me to see you again? I liked the sandwiches we found.'

'That would be lovely.' I say, privately hoping George isn't left looking after Lila for a few months, until after the wedding when we can be comfortably out of one another's lives again.

'Uncle George said he had lots of fun that day.' Lila says, absent-mindedly. 'And he didn't even buy any paper or pens or anything.'

'Maybe he liked feeding the ducks the most.' I say.

'Maybe. But he didn't feed the ducks either.'

At that moment Lila hears the theme tune of a show she enjoys on the television in the other room, and just about remembers to excuse herself politely before running out through the hallway.

I sit alone, having already set the table, hearing Nisha plating up curry and Frannie upstairs on the phone, and try not to give any meaning to Lila's words.

*

Before I know it, we are in the bright highs of summer, and it's time to return to Mijas for the wedding. I finish my last shift at Meticulous Ink before I leave, and spend some time walking aimlessly through the streets of London, feeling the thick, hot air of the city's summer against my skin, aware that the next evening I will be in the Spanish mountains, with hazy hot days and evenings like warm gentle sighs.

I pack with less care this time. Loose tops and comfortable jeans for the day, one nice skirt and camisole set in case I need to be dressed up at some point outside of the wedding day. I pull a book I want to read from my shelf, another by the French author, and toss it into my satchel, without caring much what anybody might think. Before I leave, I notice the ugly clay keepsake box on my windowsill, and quickly push it down into my bag, securing it with folded clothes, thinking that I can show Frannie the bracelet and that the clumsily made box might make her laugh.

This time I book my own flight, following Frannie and her family who will have already been there for two nights. On the plane, I feel oddly calm. This visit to Mijas will, in a lot of ways, mirror my last, in that I'm stepping in with an uncertain relationship with George, unsure how he feels or how he will react to me. But this time I'm less worried. Though things might be awkward or embarrassing, it feels as though I couldn't possibly feel any more humiliated than I did the night I went to his flat. There's nowhere to go but up. Rather than the uncertainty of last time, I'm carrying a feeling of defiance. I'm not coming for George, I never was. I'm here for Frannie, and for Theo, to make them happy and share in the joy of their day.

Mijas is as warm as ever when I step out of the airport, and I stand for a few moments in the shade. I've refused a lift, instead taking a taxi from the airport up into the mountains. The vista of the town feels different on a second viewing. Instead of the sea of whitewashed stone and terracotta roofing, I pick out the tiny details. The blue flowerpots hung from walls, with sprays of flowers, the intricate patterns on gates and window rails. The brightly coloured shop fronts set into the walls, the orange and red brocade worn by the horses who act as taxis. Viewing it the second time, I can see past the first impression, the vast expanse of white and orange, to the explosion of colour in the details, and everything is more beautiful for it.

When I walk up the drive, the first thing I see is Paloma the cat.

She stretches out in a particularly brilliant patch of sunlight and eyes me lazily, as though I had never left. I kneel down beside her, expecting her to get up and stalk away, but to my surprise she shifts her body upright, and rubs the side of her body along my knee, from nose to tail, before turning around and scenting me with the other side and returning to her spot in the sun, lifting her paw to clean it serenely with her little pink tongue.

'Wow, she likes you.' The voice is that of a young boy and I look up into Camilo's face.

'I didn't think she would say hello to me.' I try to choose my words carefully, noting the thick accent of the boy, and trying to make simple sentences. Feeling, like any true British person speaking to a child using a second language, very self-conscious about the ignorance of only speaking English.

'She doesn't like lots of people.' He bends with a hand out to Paloma, who rolls onto her belly and gently bats at his hands as he strokes the soft white fur on her stomach.

'She likes Lila now doesn't she?'

Camilo shrugs.

'Lila tried too hard. She made Paloma feel,' he pauses, sifting through his words to find what he needs, 'chased.' he settles on. 'Paloma felt she was chased, so she didn't want to be caught.'

'That's a good way of putting it,' I say, again impressed with him, and slightly sheepish at my pitiful collection of Spanish tourist phrases, 'but eventually she calmed down and now Paloma likes her?'

'I think so.' Camilo says.

'And you like her too, right?' I say.

'She is my cat.'

'No,' I smile. 'Lila, you think she's nice don't you?'

Camilo shrugs, suddenly embarrassed. 'Yes she's nice.'

I nod, but don't press further. I ask him a few questions about Mijas, whether he likes living in the town, where he lives with his mother during the rest of the year, whether he's looking forward to the wedding. Eventually, he's called back to his home. Paloma gets up to trot along behind him and I'm left crouching awkwardly over nothing on the drive and it occurs to me that I have been stretching this out, avoiding knocking on the door. Irritated with myself I straighten up and pull my case along up to the door and knock boldly, more loudly than I mean to.

When the door is answered I look into the dark, wizened face of Frannie's grandmother. I greet her in awkward Spanish, which she returns with a feeble but warm hug. I step inside and she beckons for me to put my case to one side in the hallway and then leads me through to the living room at the back. Something smells incredible, though completely unlike the Mediterranean flavours that filled the house last time I was here. As we pass the kitchen I see two women with long shiny black hair standing either side of the large cooking pot on the stove.

When we come through the plaster arch to the living room Frannie gets up from the floor, where she has been sitting with Theo and puts her arms around me.

'And that makes everyone,' Theo says, following suit. 'How was your flight?'

We exchange pleasantries while Nisha unfolds herself from the armchair where she had been reading a magazine and gives me a tight hug before sitting next to me.

'What's the incredible smell?' I ask.

'Mum's family are here now,' Nisha says, 'so we're getting the Indian family dinner experience. And if you think our Spanish family are crazy food people, you're in for a shock.'

'They brought their own spices because they didn't trust the shops here to have the right things.' Theo says.

'That's amazing.' I laugh. I look around. A few of Frannie's relatives are sitting in chairs, or dozing out on the porch. 'Where are your parents?'

'At the venue with a couple of people getting things ready and talking to the priest,' Frannie says, 'they'll be back later.'

I'm too self-conscious to ask where George is.

'And is Lila there too?' I ask.

'George took her for a walk in the town.' Nisha says, and I feel myself relax. 'There are too many people around and she was getting antsy wanting to talk to that boy.'

I remember the letter that Lila wanted to write to Camilo and wonder whether she ever quite managed to put into words what she wanted to say. I wonder if I should mention it to Nisha or Frannie, torn between wanting to respect Lila's privacy as her own person, but to protect her as a child. If Lila never actually wrote the letter, or never planned to show it to anyone, then I would be telling people something private for no reason, and betraying her trust. But if Lila was planning to bear her heart to someone, I should say something, just so Nisha can make sure she's alright.

I decide not to worry about it too much. If Lila is with George, who knows about the letter, and has known Lila all her life, then he will be in the best possible position to make that choice.

As though I've summoned them through thought, the front door opens and I hear their voices. Lila is talking animatedly and George is laughing. I brace myself as the footsteps draw closer, but it is only Lila who appears in the living room, holding a small brown bag. She cries out in delight and runs towards me, I open my arms and she jumps into them.

'I haven't seen you in ages,' she says.

'I know. I've missed you.'

My heart melts slightly, and I squeeze her a little harder, smelling the bubblegum-scented shampoo in her fawn-brown hair.

'Where did Uncle George take you?' Nisha asks, beckoning Lila to her, who walks round the table to join her. 'What have you brought back? He didn't get you some horrible little fridge magnet did he?'

'No. George says presents don't count if they're something you can eat.' Lila opens the package carefully and lifts something from the bag. I recognise it instantly as one of the powdered pastries from the cafe he and I had met at, last time we were here. This one is drizzled with lemon icing and studded with tiny blue flowers.

'Oh, you went to that little bistro in the square.' Frannie says, 'It's lovely there, I took Theo a while ago, we've been meaning to go back.'

'It's this lovely cafe,' Lila says to me, excited to share. 'Where they do pink rose drinks and green drinks and I had a hot chocolate but they put cream and strawberry sauce on it and it stirred in and melted.'

'Hydie's been there before,' George says, ducking into the room, 'we ran into each other there, last time we came out. That's how I knew you'd like it.'

Nisha pulls out the chair between her and I for George to sit on. I see him hesitate, just for a moment. He sits between us, then addresses me straight away.

'Hydie, I just took your suitcase up to your room, same one as before.'

His tone is the same, neighbourly politeness as before.

'Thank you.' I push my chair back. 'I'll quickly go and organise everything.'

'We'll shout you for dinner,' Theo calls as I leave and make my way up the stairs. I run into an auntie on the landing who hugs me and tells me I'm looking well. We chat for a few moments before she lets me go into my room.

It's unchanged from before. The strips of light across the faded carpet, the dark wooden frame of the bed and clouds of soft sheets. I slowly begin putting my things away. I'm only here for three nights. Tonight, the night of the wedding, and one more night before Frannie and Theo leave for their honeymoon. I could easily leave my clothes in the suitcase, but I carefully take out each battered pair of jeans, each faded t-shirt and hang them up. I had half-thought that George might follow me up the stairs, to try and clear the air between us. It's the sort of infuriatingly honest thing he would do. But as I line up my book, makeup and skincare on the dresser, painstakingly rearranging them for no reason at all, I realise that he instead gave me the opportunity to duck away and avoid him, and I had taken it. I wonder if I should have stayed, if I should have stubbornly kept up with the conversation and made George make the decision. But I had scarpered at the first opportunity, and now wasn't sure when I could go back down.

In an effort to give myself excuses for staying upstairs, I tip out the bag I had travelled with. Amid the receipts and SPF lip balm, hastily bought at the airport pharmacy, tumbles the wonky star-shaped box that I had packed last minute. I brighten, realising that I have a natural conversation point when I go back downstairs, an easy conversation that doesn't have to include George. I prise open the lid of the keepsake box and pull out both the bracelet and the letter, the humiliating outpouring of my heart. I hear footsteps across the hall and a gentle knock at my door. Panicking, I pull the bracelet out of the box and stuff the envelope into the pocket of my cardigan. I just pull my hand free when Frannie enters the room, and immediately sees what's in my hand.

'Is that what I think it is?' She says, slowly approaching as though I'm holding a sacred relic.

'I found it in an old box. It had been at my father's house the whole time.'

'It's fate.' Frannie says, her eyes shining with delight.

'Fate?'

'Wait there.' She says, before I can even finish my sentence. I hear her footsteps disappear down the hall then come back a few seconds before she rounds my bedroom door again. She's holding two small boxes, coated in felt. One in a rich plum, one in seafoam green. The same colour as my bridesmaid's dress.

'I was going to give it to you before the ceremony,' she says, 'but this is just too much. Hydie, open it.'

I lift the lid of the green one and have to instantly set it aside so that I can put my hand to my mouth.

It's my charm bracelet. Though not quite. It's the bracelet remade into a fine, slender piece of jewellery. The braid is now a delicate silver chain. Each charm is a sleeker, more sophisticated version of itself. At the end of the charm is a pale stone alive with dazzling rainbow light, and I realise that it is a real polished opal, Frannie's birthstone, the plastic version of which I had swapped with her for my faux amethyst all that time ago. I look up at Frannie, so full of emotion it takes me a moment to speak.

'How did you do this?'

'When I found my bracelet, I also found that notebook we kept,' she says, 'our charm swapping notebook. I got a list of every charm each of us had ever got, what we'd swapped, and then I scoured through old photos to see the order you wore it in. I don't know if it's perfect, but it's recreated as best I can.'

She opens the plum box and turns it to show me. Inside is her own bracelet recreated, this one all in gold, the amethyst plump and glossy and catching the light.

'Theo got me this as an engagement present ages ago. He knows how gutted I was to lose mine, and when I was thinking about bridesmaid's gifts, I realised that this was the only thing I wanted to give you. I hope you like it.'

'I love it,' I feel myself tearing up. Frannie waves her hands in her face.

'Don't, if you cry I'll cry.' I put my arms around her.

'Everything okay?' Theo's voice calls softly from the door. Frannie steps back and wipes her fingertips beneath her eyes.

'Everything's lovely Thee,' she says, 'just giving Frannie her present.'

'I knew she'd cry.' Theo steps inside and kisses her on the cheek, curling his hand around her upper arm. 'She's been desperate to give you that for weeks.'

'Don't put it on yet.' Frannie says, 'We'll put them on before the ceremony.'

'Sounds great.'

I hear Frannie's mother call impatiently up the stairs.

'Oh. Right,' Frannie grimaces, 'I was sent up here to get you down for dinner.'

'And I was sent to get you both when Frannie didn't reappear.'

I place the box on my dresser drawer, beside the original bracelet before following them down the steps to where the long table has been drawn out. This time it's even longer, stretching all across the dining room and out of the French windows to the patio, where every table in the house has been placed in a long row, every piece of furniture arranged around this bizarre, segmented insect, to accommodate the ludicrous amount of people now in the house.

I recognise Frannie's Indian grandparents sitting at the table. They are much older, slightly shrunken, their once-black hair now almost entirely grey, but they laugh and joke as much as they had when I last saw them. The dinner that night is a fully prepared feast of Indian food. Every baking dish, pyrex bowl and cooking pot is laid out along the table, brimming with sizzling spiced chicken dishes, paneer cheese in wilted spinach, lentil daal fragrant with aniseed and cumin, piles of flatbreads glossy with butter, and more rice than I've ever seen in my life.

'We had to borrow some pots from the neighbours,' Frannie's mum says, as she leans in to hug me hello.

'It looks incredible,' I say.

'Oh it will be,' she says, her faint Indian accent slightly thickened by time with her family. 'But I'm going to try to be somewhere else when it's time to wash up.'

Frannie's father joins the hug and for a few moments I'm squashed between them before Nisha shouts at them to let me sit down.

'She's barely off the plane, let her eat.'

She pulls out a chair between her and Frannie, at the end of the patio on garden chairs, and I quickly, gratefully rush to sit beside her, noting George sitting down beside his Indian grandmother who beams at him and tussles his hair like he's a child still. Lila has been pulled from her own seat onto her Grandfather's lap, and is glowing with pride as she tells him about school and he lavishes her with praise. Theo is three seats down from Frannie, with his own mother and father, a Japanese couple who speak perfect English but no Spanish, but are nevertheless chatting animatedly to Frannie's aunts who speak limited English, with the help of exaggerated miming.

The food is somehow even better than it looks. I had grown up spoiled by Frannie's mother's cooking, and I shamelessly lean across the table trying to pull a bit of everything onto my plate.

'You can tell Mum made the chapatis,' Nisha says biting into a thin flatbread and moaning in delight, 'Nobody does them like her.'

I look at the enormous family around me, the different cultures blurring together. Frannie's Spanish grandmother brandishing a spoonful of something red, and glossy with tomatoes, at her Indian Uncle, who, with the help of Frannie's father, is explaining the recipe. The grandmother downs the spoonful with delight and double dips the serving spoon straight back into the dish while Frannie's father puts his head in his hands to hide his laughter.

Frannie had joked with me privately about her decision to marry Theo, and how she had, though not deliberately, chosen a man with whom she would have children who would be British, Spanish, Indian and Japanese all in one. I felt, as I often did with her family, just a little bereft. Sitting among people all so tightly and lovingly connected, even if they had never met, because the people they loved, loved one another. I felt, as I often did, adrift from this. As though the threads that once tied me to other people had come loose and fallen away a long time ago. I could love my parents for the people they were, but it did not replace what I felt from Frannie's family, love amplified and magnified, given and received over and over again, even when there were arguments, even when there was tension. To be in a family like this was to be endlessly loved, and to love in return, in infinite directions all at once.

I feel myself being watched and I look up instinctively, to see George quickly turn his head away. I realise I've been staring ahead as I've been musing. I shake myself off and tune into the conversation with Nisha and an Indian auntie.

'She's growing up faster than I expected.' Nisha is saying, looking over at her daughter who is now soberly nodding along to a discussion George is having. 'She's got a little crush on that kid across the road.'

'Camilo?'

'She tries to keep it secret but you know how kids are.'

'Camilo's a good boy,' the aunt says, 'she could do worse.'

Nisha is thoughtful, poking at her food with a fork. 'I just don't want her embarrassing herself in front of him. An experience like that can scar a kid. She's so clever and kind. I don't want her feeling bad about herself because of some boy.'

'Oh Nisha,' the auntie shakes her head, 'what are those years for if not for embarrassing yourself while you're young enough to not be hardened by it?'

'I suppose that's part of being a mother,' Nisha says. 'You know your kid will have to experience some kind of pain sooner or later, but you try to make sure they avoid it for as long as possible, even if that would make things worse in the long run.'

The auntie puts a hand, perfectly manicured in cocoa-coloured polish, on Nisha's arm. 'She will be okay, so long as she knows that you'll be there for her, whatever happens.'

CHAPTER EIGHTEEN

After the meal is finished I make sure I volunteer to help clear up. Frannie tries to lure me away to the balcony but I insist, having not helped at all either setting up the table or cooking the food. I collect plates and cutlery as people move around me to other parts of the house, some wandering into the garden and others going into the living room, or to sit out at the front.

I help the men pull chairs and tables back to where they belong and return to the kitchen to help with the dishes. To my surprise, many of the large pots have already been washed, and are drying on dishcloths that have been laid on the counter. At the sink I see George, who has started on the large stack of plates, carefully scrubbing at each in the water.

He hasn't noticed me yet. It is just he and I alone and I stand in the doorway, unsure of myself. He has a look of serious concentration on his face as he scrubs away at the dish in his hands, the wet edge of the sink leaving a tiny line of water on the pale grey fabric of his shirt.

'Hi,' I say, suddenly aware of how bizarre it would be to just stand there, staring at him.

'Oh,' he looks round, his face, which usually breaks into a wide friendly grin whenever he sees me, is now cautious and slightly sheepish. 'Hi, did you enjoy dinner?'

'It was really good,' I say, 'I just wanted to help clear up as I didn't contribute to anything else.'

'Me neither,' George says, 'but I've got this. If you want to go and keep Frannie company I can finish up.'

I scan along the counter. He's running out of room. Wet dishes are already balancing precariously against one another on his makeshift drying rack.

'Let me at least help clear this.' I say. I'm surprised by my own boldness, but I realise that when George is confident and accommodating, I take refuge in my own shyness. In the face of George being awkward, I find that I have the space to be assertive. I take a handful of clean, folded dishcloths from a basket on the counter and begin to dry off the large cooking pots and dishes.

'Thanks,' he says, as I open the cupboards, looking for the right places to put things. 'I think that was all a disaster waiting to happen.' I don't look up but I hear him pause, and take a deep breath before talking again.

Speaking of disasters,' he says. 'I want to apologise again about that night a while ago. It was fun and I ruined it.'

I can't help but laugh at him, speaking quickly when he looks put out. 'Nice segue,' I say, 'it's okay. Though Frannie tells me you've finally come clean about the breakup?'

George smiles. 'Yes. I'm not sure why I held off so long. In the end they were weirder about it than they would have been in the first place.'

'Well, that's always the way isn't it?' I say, getting to work drying a stubbornly damp cast iron pot. 'If you try to avoid something because you're scared of it, you just end up running into a worse version later on.'

'Very true.' George says. 'The quicker you face whatever's happened, the easier it is.'

We lapse into silence, the stop and start of the tap, and the clinking of crockery substituting the rest of that conversation that we both know we should have. I crouch to open a low cupboard and carefully stack pans in size order, kneeling on the floor to reach inside. I can feel him wanting to talk about the last night we were together, and I cast around for a topic to manoeuvre us away from that subject. I open my mouth, planning to ask about the wedding tomorrow, but before I can say a word he turns, his face resolute, and says:

'Is that why we never talked about Frannie's birthday?'

I stare, completely stunned, looking up at him from the floor as though I've been hit in the face. He watches me for a beat.

'Don't look at me like that. Is that why you spent ten years avoiding me?'

For a few moments I reel at the moment that has finally come, out of the blue. And then something surfaces in my mind, and I realise the truth.

'That night,' I say, 'that night when we went back to yours. You didn't pull away because of some anxiety over my age. Or about Frannie, or even your breakup. You pulled away because of what happened all that time ago.'

He presses his lips together and I know I'm right.

'That was years ago,' I say, standing up, trying to keep my voice level.

'And yet it's hung over every second we've spent together since,' George says, 'not that there have been many as you literally evaporated afterwards.'

'Because I was humiliated,' I say, 'because I was a little kid who'd just completely bared her soul to someone who'd said no.'

'Of course I said no.' George says, looking offended. 'You were a child, what was I going to do? I tried to be as kind as I could. But there was no way of getting out of that without you being hurt.'

'I know that,' I say, 'And I understand that you were as kind as you could have been.'

'So why did you disappear?' he asks, and I'm surprised to hear the hurt in his voice. It must show on my face because he crosses his arms defensively. 'You weren't just Frannie's friend you know,' he says. 'Just because you were a kid doesn't mean I didn't care about you. You were still important to me. I saw how much you needed our family, and suddenly you just stopped being there. And it was my fault. I thought I'd pushed you away and now you were all on your own again.'

'God, I'm so sorry,' I say sarcastically, 'I'm so sorry that *you* felt bad about it. You're right, how you feel about this is the important thing here.'

'I'm not saying that,' he snaps, 'I'm saying you're not the only person who's been carrying this round, wondering whether to bring it up. And when you were at mine I realised I couldn't push it away any longer.' He sighs. 'I should have brought it up before anything happened. But how do you talk about something like that after all this time?'

I don't know what to say. On the one hand, it's as though a pressure valve has been released, a build-up of feeling I didn't know I was holding is dissipating, but on the other, this conversation has caught me so unprepared for it, that any relief I feel is being eaten by a trembling sense of uncertainty about where we go from here. My new experiences with George had given me so much to think about that the old memories had started to feel like background noise. I had almost gotten used to them. It hadn't occurred to me that George had been thinking about them all this time.

'Are you two alright?' Frannie asks from the doorway. We both jump and turn to her. 'Am I catching you two having one of your little kitchen dialogues?'

'Everything's fine,' I say, feigning brightness. George also switches on a smile.

'Just complaining that we're the only people who thought to do a bit of clearing up.'

'Piss off,' Frannie laughs, 'I'm about to wave off Theo and the others staying in the hotel. Come say goodbye.'

Frannie marches in and helps us clear away the last few things, then we follow her in silence to the front of the house where all the families are crowded in the garden. Theo is holding his mother's hand, and a gaggle of other relatives including Nisha and Lila have already started to make their way down the steps to the centre of town, where they'll make their way across to the large hotel on the outskirts. Frannie's Spanish relatives are leaving for their own homes, or crossing the road to the neighbour's house, where Camilo's family will put them up for the night.

'See you tomorrow.' Frannie says to Theo. She pulls him into a kiss, then pulls away laughing when somebody whistles. Theo waves to the crowd who cheer him off as he leads his parents away for the night, surrounded by a bustling crowd of his soon-to-be family.

'Right,' Frannie says, checking the time on her phone, 'what do you reckon? One last look at the moon as an unmarried woman?'

She takes mine and George's silence as agreement and leads us back through to the garden. The house, which was so full of people it was stifling just a few moments ago, has emptied so suddenly that it's eerie. I hear shuffling above us of Frannie's parents and grandparents going to bed and then it's just me, Frannie and George, stepping out in our bare feet onto the smooth cool patio and sitting on the wide base of the French windows.

Frannie looks up at the sky, the moon full and bright and the clear mountain air scattered with stars. I watch her, her face so contented, like a woman about to open a door she's been wanting to step through her whole life. I can't imagine what it would be like to ever feel so sure of my choices. I often wonder if it's the difference in our upbringings, or if there's some kind of gene that allows some people to stride into the unknown with complete confidence that they're going in the right direction. By instinct I look up and meet George's eyes. He has been watching me while I've been watching Frannie. He gives me a small smile which I return, and we both turn our heads to the sky. I feel like we've silently agreed to a truce, to table whatever discussion we need to have until after the wedding.

'Isn't it scary?' I ask, unable to help myself. 'Tomorrow you'll do something that will change the rest of your life. How can you be sure you're making the right choice'

Frannie is silent, and for a moment I tense, worried I've offended her.

'The thing is,' Frannie says slowly, as though she is writing the words out carefully in the air. 'I don't think you should live your life thinking about whether you're doing the right thing. You should try to be a good person. But there are no right choices, there's only what you do in the moment. You can weigh your options and agonise over consequences as much as you like, but at the end of the day, you always have to move ahead without knowing how things will turn out. Maybe Theo and I will live happily ever after, maybe we'll crash and burn and be divorced this time next year.'

'Mum would murder you both,' George murmurs.

'But it will probably be somewhere in between. We'll have good moments and bad moments, and things will happen that will fill us with joy and sometimes we'll let each other down. But if we don't make choices that force us into the unknown, we don't get to create new paths for ourselves and discover what that life could look like.'

'I'm sold,' George says, looking out at the sky, 'I'll call Rowena and ask her.'

Frannie snorts and the two of them fall about laughing.

'You will not.' Frannie says. 'You took that step and realised you weren't happy. Things never felt right.'

'It's hard to know what the right feelings are supposed to be sometimes.' he says. I hear a tinge of sadness in his voice. I want to reach for his hand, to touch the side of his face and comfort him. But I don't move.

Frannie shifts her weight to tuck her arm into his.

'The right person will feel like the right person,' she says, 'and I feel like that's different for everyone. But with Theo, things have always been new and familiar at the same time. I've only known him a few years, but it feels as though he fits my whole life up to this point. Like he belongs in my past even though he wasn't there. Does that make sense?'

'I don't know. But it sounds very wise.' George says.

'I am very wise. Sometimes I forget I'm the youngest child.' Frannie says smugly.

'I don't,' George replies, 'they're always the most irritating.'

Frannie laughs again and shoves him with her elbow.

They talk about silly things, memories from childhood. Some I had been there for and some I hadn't, but I'm content to sit and listen to them. Eventually the chatter slows, and Frannie looks at the time on her phone.

'We should sleep,' she says, getting to her feet, 'I don't want to oversleep for my own wedding.' We all stand and step back into the dark, quiet house.

'Thanks, you two.' Frannie turns to us when we reach the landing. I'm conscious of the distance between me and George as I feel her taking us both in, standing as we are together. 'I'll see you in the morning.'

She goes into her room first, leaving us in awkward silence, the lynchpin of Frannie being removed leaving room for the earlier tension to flood back in. I pause with my hand on my bedroom door, wondering if I should say goodnight to George. He too pauses, and for just a beat we stand at each end of the hall, mirroring one another. I begin pushing open the door when I hear him take a breath, as though to speak, but I have already stepped through before I realise what I'm hearing, and the door shuts softly behind me, leaving only silence.

*

I wake to my alarm, set to a low volume and tucked beneath my pillow so as not to disturb others. I had gotten into bed with a racing mind, but had fallen asleep almost immediately. The morning is still pale and cool, and I enjoy a few moments of peace and silence. In a few hours we will be picked up by taxis to take us to the hotel, Frannie, her mother, Nisha, Lila and I will get ready there and be driven back up the chapel. Her father, Theo, George, and the rest of the families will join us there. When the ceremony is complete we will pile back into cars and drive down to the hotel again, where we will eat and have the reception. The day will be full of people, food and drink, laughing and dancing, and I enjoy the time spent lying by myself in the silence before it all starts.

I read in bed for almost an hour before I hear other doors opening, a shower turning on, murmurs from the ground floor and the balcony as people begin to get ready. I put on jeans and a plain camisole and sling on the same cardigan I wore the day before. I brush my hair and put on just enough makeup to feel presentable. The dresses are all at the hotel, and there will be a stylist for makeup and hair when we get there. Downstairs I find Frannie and her mother standing in the kitchen. Frannie's mother is holding her hand and I hesitate, feeling as though I'm intruding, but they turn to me before I can move back out of sight. Frannie smiles when she sees me. She's wearing the beautiful loose plum trouser suit she showed me at her house, her hair down and her skin makeup-free and golden.

'Good morning love.' Frannie's mother greets me, and pulls out a chair at the little round table. 'How did you sleep?'

I greet her as Frannie gets up to make coffee.

'Where is everyone else?' I ask.

'Abuela is changing upstairs. Dad, George and Abuelo went straight to the hotel.' Frannie says 'It's easier for them to all change and get ready there, rather than everyone queueing for the bathroom here. Nisha and Lila are there as well, so they should be ready before we arrive.'

'All smartly thought out,' Frannie's mum says, 'and gets people out of the way so we can have some peace before we go down there.'

I nod. Frannie brings the pot of coffee across to the table with a small jug of milk, and I get up before her mother can and pull three mugs from the cupboards.

'Bring another if you can,' Frannie calls, 'Abuela will want one'

I dig out another and, holding them ungracefully, make my way to the table.

'I hope you're more adept at holding a bouquet.' Frannie laughs as she pours coffee into each mug. Her mother picks up the milk jug and pours a thin spiral into Frannie's, a more generous helping into mine, and somewhere between into her own.

'Perhaps you take more now,' she smiles at me, 'but this is the coffee you would have when we had our pastry mornings on Saturdays. Do you remember?'

'Of course,' I say, 'it was the first time I ever had coffee. I still take it this way, lots of milk and no sugar.'

I'm warmed that she remembers exactly the amount of milk that I take in my coffee. I'm about to ask if she remembers all our pastry orders too, a plain croissant for her, an almond croissant for me, and a pain au chocolat for Frannie, when her phone buzzes from the pocket of the jacket she's hung on the chair. As she reaches around for it I realise that Frannie's phone on the table has also lit up.

'Who's calling you?' Frannie says picking up her own phone.

'It's Nisha,' Sameera says, 'you?'

'Theo. What about you?'

She's talking to me, and I look down at the table where my phone is showing an incoming call. George is ringing me.

'Oh for god's sake,' Frannie says, 'something's obviously gone wrong.' She holds the phone to her ear as her mother answers her call.

I pick up my phone as I hear Frannie go 'I don't think this counts as seeing me before the wedding but this had better be important.'

'George?' I say into the phone, looking over at Frannie's mum, who brings a hand to her mouth.

'Hydie?' he says.

'What's going on? Everyone's phones are ringing.'

'Are you still at the house? Is Frannie still there?'

'Yes, we're all still here, what's happened?'

Somehow even as George begins to explain, I already know. There's only one thing that could be happening to cause such a panic. Frannie's mother grips the phone in both hands and begins shouting questions down the phone frantically at Nisha,

Frannie has already hung up and has run to the hallway, I hear her picking up keys and pulling on her shoes. Shouting up the stairs in Spanish to her grandmother.

'We'll all be there, we're coming as soon as we can.' I say to George and hang up, stuffing the phone in my pocket as Frannie runs back in. We all stare at one another. We all know what's happened, but none of us wants to say it, to say words that will shatter the quiet calm of the morning. Lila is missing.

CHAPTER NINETEEN

The quiet morning outside the hotel ends at its glass sliding doors. There is chaos inside, people from all sides of the family and hotel staff running around, talking in frantic groups. Even tourists who have nothing to do with the family seem to be helping out. A printed picture of Lila is being handed around.

At reception, we find Nisha, wide-eyed and so pale her tan skin has gone grey.

'We're here,' her mother says, pulling her into a strong hug, 'what happened?'

'Oh God,' she whispers. She looks as though she's going to be sick. 'I don't know. I don't know.'

'Nisha, where did you see her last?' Frannie runs to her 'Where have you checked?'

'You need to be getting ready for the wedding' Nisha says, 'Theo's round here somewhere, he can't see you.'

'Nisha shut up. Nothing's happening until we find Lila.'

Nisha doesn't look as though she's going to cry, she looks beyond crying, hollowed out with panic. She swallows and speaks again.

'We were together for breakfast. Some of the family went up to the chapel to make sure the venue was all fine and to see if Theo needed anything. I thought she'd gone down with them, I assumed she went with George. But then I found this,' she pulls a silver thin silver hairband from her pocket. 'It's for her hair. I called George to tell her she'd forgotten it, and he said she didn't go with them. And she's not with anyone else I've called. I don't know where she's gone.'

Nisha's breath begins to hitch and her mother catches her hand and rubs her back as Nisha presses her collarbone hard with her hand.

'Right,' Frannie says, 'this is absolute madness right now. We need people stationed in places around the hotel, the chapel and the town rather than everyone just running around.'

She takes a photo of Lila on the reception desk and turns it over, pulling a pen from the pot and beckoning a receptionist over.

'You three,' she gestures to her mum and two of the hotel staff who have come to talk to us. 'We need to be organised.' She begins to write down the initials of everyone at the wedding, splitting them into groups along lines of family and friends and first languages, then assigning each of them search tasks and places to check; the foyer, the gardens, knocking on room doors on different floors. As she's scribbling, Theo and George emerge from a corridor and hurry towards us.

The look Nisha gives them breaks my heart, the strangled hope, quickly followed by a fresh wave of utter panic when they shake their heads.

'Here,' Frannie hands the list over to Sameera and the members of staff. 'Each of you take a photo of this list on your phone and go around making sure everyone knows where they should be. I'm going to print more photos and take them to people in the town near here. Someone might have seen her or taken her in. Theo come with me, then when you've got the pictures, round up everyone you can and get them to walk different ways back up towards the house in case she's lost somewhere there.' Theo nods, his face grim.

'And you two,' she says, pushing a handful of the pictures into George's hands, 'you're on free-roaming duty. I want you guys checking all the spaces in between the rooms, corridors, lifts, stairwells, the path between here and the chapel, anywhere I haven't thought of here.'

'We'll find her Nishio,' George says, using a name I haven't heard him use since he and his sister were teenagers, 'she'll be fine, she'll be back in no time and you can get on with telling her off.'

Nisha can't bring herself to react, just nods mutely and allows herself to be steered away by her mother as she and the hotel staff begin to hurry to the back of the hotel, to the restaurant and gardens.

'God she looks awful.' Frannie says. She turns to me, George and Theo. 'Everyone else is going to be a state.' she says 'You can see it. I need us four to hold it together completely. We don't panic, we don't get overwhelmed. We focus up and we find Lila okay?'

The three of us nod, all wearing looks of absolute focus. I push down the panic I feel, all the horrible scenarios conjured by the idea of a missing child.

'We'll find her,' George says again, as though trying to will the idea into existence.

'Let's go.' Frannie and Theo turn and stride back to the reception area, where the receptionist is printing out more photos of Lila.

'Stairs first?' I ask.

'As good a place as any.' George says. He writes awkwardly on the back of his photo of Lila, I see him listing in-between spaces as Frannie had said. 'This way we can keep track of where we've checked.'

'We shouldn't go together,' I say, 'we should look on our own.'

'Really?' George gives me a withering look 'You can't put our issues aside for Lila?'

'That's not what I mean,' I say, keeping my voice calm, understanding that George is immensely stressed. 'I mean that if Lila's in an in-between space, she's probably not standing there, is she? She'll be moving through it, either looking for someone or -' I hesitate, the words *with someone* hang unsaid in the air and we both try not to acknowledge it. I continue quickly. 'If we stagger our checking we've got double the chance of finding her.'

George's expression softens. 'You're completely right.' he says. 'I'm so sorry, I just-'

'It's fine,' I reassure him, lifting a hand to his arm and squeezing it gently, 'let's just get her found and then things can go back to being awkward.'

He nods. We write out our list of places to check and decide that he will start from the top, and I will start a few places down the list, so he will be around fifteen minutes behind me.

'And if you see anything, let me know.'

I nod and set off to the gardens, while George walks the other way to the lifts. I force myself to stay calm as I climb down the patio steps, calling out Lila's name. I hear other members of the family doing the same in the distance, Lila's name echoing around the hotel gardens like bird calls. I do a lap of the path that goes around the hotel, the corridor of each of the four floors, walk through every hall on the ground floor and check the car park, with absolutely no sign of Lila. I message George each time I move through an area on the list. He doesn't reply, presumably following my trail with increased desperation. Frannie and Nisha both ring me once, checking in, each sounding frantic. After an hour, nobody has found her.

After I've cleared all the areas in the hotel I follow the steps back out to the front, where I can see the chapel up in the distance, up the mountains past the town. The sun is high and hot in the sky, and I take my cardigan off, wrapping it around my waist. Something falls to the floor, and as I pick it up I see that it's the letter I wrote to George, that I'd stuffed quickly into my pocket the night before. I fold it small and tuck it into the pocket of my jeans before starting the walk up the hill. I see the priest from the chapel, and a stocky blonde man I recognise as Theo's best man, handing out the photos of Lila printed from the hotel to people from the town. The priest is already in his full vestments for the wedding, and is so old he seems stooped under the weight of it.

From where I am, up in the path carved into the side of the mountain I had a reasonable view of Mijas Pueblo. I scan out across the town, looking for a head of shiny light brown hair, a pink flower girl dress. I try not to think about seeing her being led away by a stranger, or being pulled into a car, stood so far away, with no power to stop it. I turn away from the view feeling sick. All I can do is search the areas I've been given, and pray that someone calls me soon.

Looking back at the path, something catches my eye, crumpled and red beneath a scrubby bush. I crouch and pull it from under the dusty branches. I immediately recognise the thick red paper and can't work out why, but as I unfold it I realise it's an envelope - the envelope that Lila bought from the stationers - the envelope from the letter she was planning to write to Camilo. I dig my phone out of my pocket and send a picture to George.

Is Camilo at the hotel yet? I ask. He replies immediately.

His family went back to his house in case she comes back. And then a second later, *Shit is that the paper she bought at your work?*

Find Camilo, I say, *He might know where she is.*

I put my phone back in my pocket and keep climbing to the chapel, the last stop on my list. My last hope. The doors are flung open and the church is abandoned, the priest, the photographer and church staff having all left to join the search. Lila is not here. The chapel has been decorated beautifully for the wedding, the wooden pews frothing with white and lilac flowers, the altar and walls hung with shimmering cloths in pale gold that catch the light falling through the window. It looks like something from a Medieval fairy tale and for just a moment I stop and take a breath at the sheer beauty of the place. Despite my panic, something in me responds to the feeling of being somewhere cool and quiet in all the commotion. I touch the flowers of the back pew, running my fingers along the soft petals.

I move out of the back of the chapel and into the garden. It feels more lush and tropical than when I was last there, the flowers heavy and lounging in the sun. I reach the gate at the back of the paving, remembering Lila jumping up and down to see beyond it, and that behind the gate is the pool. And I know, without knowing why I know it, that Lila is there. Panic grips me and I run the last few feet, sprinting through the gate, prepared to jump into the water, dreading the worst.

She is sitting on the white stone steps beside the pool in her bridesmaid's dress, her hair carefully combed and styled with flowers, clutching a pink piece of paper. She has pulled her shoes off and thrown them into a corner where they've landed clumsily in a pile.

'Lila,' I say. She looks up and I see that her face is flushed and red with dried tears. As I approach she sees the red envelope in my hand and begins to cry again. I sit beside her.

'I think this belongs to you.' I say softly, holding the envelope out to her.

'I don't want it.' Her raw voice is heartbreaking. 'It's so stupid.'

'Did you give it to Camilo?' I ask, knowing that I'm right.

She sniffs and nods her head, staring out at the dancing light on the surface of the pool.

'I asked him to read it and he did.'

'Then what?' Her lip trembles and I put my arm around her. She's so small in the crook of my elbow. 'Don't worry. You don't have to tell me.'

'I'm so stupid,' she says under her breath.

'No,' I say strongly squeezing her tightly, 'you're not.'

'I feel stupid,' she says.

I stroke the top of her head with one hand while reaching into my pocket with the other. My fingers find the hastily folded letter.

'Do you want to read something that will make you feel better?' I ask.

She looks up at me curiously and I unfold the envelope, pulling out the letter, yellowed with age.

'I was a bit older than you when I wrote this,' I say, 'And I never gave it to him, but I know how brave you have to be to write something like this.'

She takes it and, to my surprise, offers me hers. I accept, holding it in my lap. We read for a few minutes in silence. The letter hurts to read, her innocence, the earnestness of her feelings, but mostly the familiarity of it all. I recognise so clearly all the hope she was carrying in her letter, the warm glittering ideal of a boy she didn't really know at all. I wait for her to finish mine.

'Well?' I ask.

'Your handwriting was rubbish,' she says, a glimpse of a cheeky smile on her tear-stained face. I laugh.

'No, your handwriting is just really nice,' I say.

'But it's nice,' she says, 'It's sweet that you think all these things about Uncle George.'

'Well, I wrote that when I was much younger,' I say, 'My point is that you're not stupid for feeling this way, and you're not stupid for telling him. You're incredibly brave. It hurts when someone doesn't like us back the way we want them to, but that doesn't mean you shouldn't have told them .'

A creak sounds at the gate and we both look up to see George, dark curls plastered to his face, wedding shirt creased from running. He looks at Lila, then at me, and doubles over with his face in his hands, audibly gasping in relief. I smile.

'Can you message Nisha, Frannie and your Mum? They'll tell everyone else.'

He nods and walks across to us, pulling out his phone. He sits on the other side of Lila, who tears up again at the sight of him.

'I'm so sorry,' she begins but he interrupts her.

'You're safe,' he says, 'that's all that matters. What are you holding?' he asks, looking down at his phone as he begins to type.

Lila looks at me and must see the panic in my face because she quickly hands it back to me and takes back her own letter.

'I gave Camilo the letter I wrote,' she said, lifting her chin in the air, trying to seem unfazed. 'but he doesn't like me back the way I want him to.'

George finishes typing and puts his phone in his pocket. Silently he puts his arm around her and kisses the top of her head, fiercely.

I take Lila's hand, so small in mine.

'He should be flattered that someone as wonderful as you would feel that way about him,' I say.

'Yeah,' she smiles, 'he should.' She crumples up her letter and gives me a look. I crumple up mine.

'Here's to being a stupid little girl,' I say, and lob my letter into the pool. It's swiftly followed by hers, and the two darken as they become waterlogged, the paper turning to pulp and sinking.

'Is my Mum really mad at me?' Lila asks us.

'I think right now she'll just be happy you're safe.' George gets to his feet, 'But I'd make sure you keep your room extra clean for a few weeks.'

Lila nods and takes the hand that he offers to her, pulling on his weight as she gets to her feet. I stand up also. The letters are shrunken and dark, as small as faraway planets, at the bottom of the water. There was something cleansing about it. I hope it felt as good for Lila as it did to me, to have taken ownership of her feelings and have let them go.

'I've told your Mum we'll meet them at the chapel.' George says. 'Let's go.'

Still holding her hand he leads her carefully out around the pool and across the garden. When we step back into the church we hear an anguished cry and look through to the front doors, where Nisha is running up the steps, having spotted us from where she was climbing.

George lets go of Lila's hands as she runs to her mother who falls to her knees to catch her in her arms in the middle of the aisle. A few petals fall from the pews to land on the mother and daughter as they embrace, Nisha weeping uncontrollably, her hand held tight against the back of her daughter's head.

'Oh thank God,' I hear Theo's voice and look up to see him, Frannie and the priest entering the church. The priest claps his hand to his mouth in relief and Theo looks as though he might fold over onto the floor. Frannie strides across, seemingly unflappable, but falters as Lila pulls away from her mother and buries her head against the fabric of her silken plum suit.

'I ruined your wedding,' she whispers, 'I'm so sorry.'

Frannie takes her in her arms, holds her tight, as though afraid she might vanish again.

'It doesn't matter,' she says, and I realise she is crying. 'As long as you're safe. It doesn't matter at all.'

The priest says something in Spanish and Theo replies in kind. He didn't speak Spanish when I first met him, he has learned it for Frannie.

'I know, I know,' Frannie says, 'but what were we supposed to do?' She speaks in Spanish with the priest and everyone but me turns to listen.

George takes a few steps until he is beside me and leans in, so close I feel the warmth of him against me.

'The wedding should have started over an hour ago.' he murmurs. 'We won't be back to the hotel in time for the caterers unless we eat before the wedding, but the reception room won't be ready.'

I nod, watching as Frannie takes out her phone and Theo does the same.

'Right, team,' she pulls a piece of paper out of her pocket, 'here are all the groups we made for search parties, everyone on the guest list is written here. If we each call two people from the group and get them to round up everyone else, everyone can be here in the next thirty minutes. We'll send taxis to collect anyone who needs them and once everyone's here we'll just get started. I've just messaged the hotel to send the caterers home so we don't need to worry about food. We'll get the ceremony done, have a quick drink in the garden while we get photos, and send everyone off into town to find their own dinner. Half of them are Spanish, they barely eat before nine anyway. We'll collect the cake from the hotel tomorrow and people can eat it at the house.'

'Aren't you going to get ready?' Nisha asks, looking at

Frannie's outfit.

'I would rather wear this and just get on with things.' she says. 'So long as neither of you mind?' She looks at Theo and the Priest who both shake their heads.

'I don't have anyone's number,' I say. 'Why don't I go back and collect anything we might need from the hotel?'

'Get your dress,' Frannie says, 'and Nisha's. Don't worry about mine, there isn't time.'

'We don't want to upstage you,' Nisha says, recovering her usual poise, though she still holds tight to Lila's hand.

'Please,' Frannie raises an eyebrow and gestures at her suit, 'look at me, you won't.' Everyone laughs but the Priest, who looks bemused until Theo gives him a quick translation.

After a brief discussion to confirm our plans, George and I set off from the chapel, walking back down the hill.

'Are you not on call duty?' I ask.

'I'm going to sort the taxis, I'll get one up to collect Abuela and anyone still back at the house, then go down and collect you along with anyone who needs a lift.'

'That is handy,' I say, 'I wasn't looking forward to lugging a load of clothes up that hill.'

'Get going and I'll meet you out at the front of the hotel.'

We part as he pulls his phone out of his pocket and I begin to rush back down the hill. On my way I come across the group of locals who had been talking to the priest earlier, someone shouts to me.

'Did you find the little girl?'

With no time to stop I just give them two thumbs up, which they receive with a loud cheer, then have to hurry past them to the bottom of the hill and quickly back to the hotel. I tell the receptionist to take down the printed photos of Lila, to which she gives a cry of relief. Then I rush to the room where Frannie and her bridal party would have been getting ready.

I don't have much time to stop and appreciate the dressing room full of beautiful furnishings, vanity mirrors and flock wallpaper. Two champagne bottles are sat in a bucket of what was once ice but is now tepid water, and most of the stylist's tools are left spilling out of a bag on the floor, Frannie having called her to bring some hairspray, a brush and what makeup she could carry up the hill as quickly as she can. I pull the bridesmaid dresses in their bags, feeling grateful I don't have to take responsibility for Frannie's dress, which is beautiful but heavy and ornate, and has a long delicate train and veil that I would almost certainly step on if I had to carry it by myself.

I rush back out and see a taxi waiting, with George stood outside.

'Everyone else has been delivered,' he says with a smile. 'Just you and me kiddo.'

I gratefully allow him to lift the dresses from me and lie them carefully in the back of the taxi.

'Wait, come with me,' I say, and run back inside.

'We don't have much time,' he calls after me, but runs through the lobby after me anyway. When he gets to the dressing room he sees me beginning to lift Frannie's wedding dress from the railing.

'Brilliant idea,' he says, and takes the end, so we can carry it off the ground between us, me holding the hanger, him holding the train.

'Frannie can put it on for the photos in the garden,' I say, 'it seems a shame to leave it hanging there.'

We place it in the back seat of the taxi with the care of someone laying down an ancient, crumbling artefact.

I climb in beside it, holding the other dresses in my lap and George gets in the front. The taxi driver takes us right to the door of the chapel. George pays him as I begin to carefully lift the dresses and jewellery out of the car. He hurries to help with them when Theo comes out of the chapel.

'Oi,' George yells, 'look away!' Theo spots the pile of white fabric and panics, turning around and staring stupidly at the wall.

'I didn't think you were bringing it,' he said.

'Neither did I but Hydie was determined.'

'Where is Frannie?' I ask.

'In the little bit where the bridal party are supposed to wait so the groom doesn't see them,' he says, shuffling round to avoid looking at the dress as we walk past, 'as if we haven't spent the last two hours running around with each other. But tradition is tradition, I suppose.'

We get past him and quietly move along the back of the chapel, trying to avoid the guests seeing us. The church is packed, every row is filled to bursting with Frannie and Theo's families, and some of their friends who had flown in that afternoon for the reception, but were now in time to attend the whole thing.

We go through a small wooden door and find Frannie and her father, along with Nisha and Lila in a warm, cramped room where a stylist is dabbing gloss onto Frannie's lips.

Frannie looks up at her brother who walks ahead of me.

'George you'll have to stay out, there's not enough room for more people in he-' she falters, as I follow him, her wedding dress coming into view. 'You brought it up' she says.

'There's probably no time to put it on now,' I say, 'but let's come back here and get you into it for the evening.'

Nisha stands up and pushes past her, back to her old self. She grabs the two bridesmaid dresses from George and presses one into my chest.

'No time,' she says. 'Change, now. Men out.'

The two men and Lila vacate the room and Nisha and I quickly pull off our clothes and slip into the dresses. The stylist quickly dusts our faces with powder and applies mascara and shimmering highlighter to each of us. Before she leaves she hands me a brush which I hastily pull through my hair as Nisha tucks her short hair behind her ears.

'You both look beautiful,' Frannie says, and turns me round away from her, quickly and carefully weaving my hair into the loose braid her mother would do for me when I was young. She turns me back to face her, pulling out a few pieces of hair which frame my face. Nisha steps in and puts her arms around both of us. She's never hugged me tightly before, and I feel the firm squeeze of her fingers around my shoulder as she kisses us both gently on the cheek. Frannie puts her arms around us both and I do the same, and we stand for a few moments in a silent embrace until a quiet knock sounds from the other side of the door and we separate. Nisha opens the door for Frannie who steps outside. I follow and Nisha closes the door behind us.

Frannie's father is almost in tears the second he lays eyes on her. He puts his hands tight against his mouth and shakes his head, apparently lost for words. Frannie laughs and puts her arms around him.

'Dad I've been wearing this the whole day.'

He takes the pocket square from his suit and quickly dabs at his eyes.

'I know,' he says, 'but you were gone for five minutes and I forgot how beautiful you looked.'

I catch Lila rolling her eyes and have to press my lips together to keep from laughing.

George pokes his head back around to speak to us.

'They're ready when you are,' he says, 'you look beautiful.'

I turn to smile at the group, and my heart jumps when I realise that he is looking straight at me.

'You know you can say that to all of us if you like,' Nisha says slyly, and George shoots her a look. I realise he's embarrassed, and I spare him by catching Frannie's eye and smiling, pretending I haven't heard any of it.

'One last thing,' Frannie says. She ducks back into the room and brings out the jewellery boxes our bracelets are in. 'I got Abuela to bring these from the house when we collected her.' She opens the cases and I see both her and my new bracelets, slender and beautiful. And nestled within them, the original charm bracelets, chunkier, less expensive looking, but still beautiful in their own way.

Frannie puts my new bracelet on my wrist, and hers on her own. Then she lifts out the originals and puts them on Nisha and Lila. They were sized for children, so Frannie's old bracelet just fits on Nisha's adult wrist, clasped at the last link in the chain. Mine fits Lila perfectly.

'We're ready.' Frannie says.

'Good. On the music.' George gives her hand a squeeze and leaves, his footsteps fading as he walks back up the altar to where Theo is standing with his best man. We shuffle into formation. Lila is at the front with a basket of dried flowers, me and Nisha behind her, and Frannie and her father at the back. The piano starts the traditional Bridal Chorus song, and Nisha gently pushes Lila in the back.

'Not too quickly,' she whispers, and Lila steps out and walks carefully up the aisle, casting the flowers in arcs across the flagstone floor. I see Camilo and his family in the aisle and watch as Lila gives him a friendly smile before walking past, scattering petals elegantly, her little head held high.

Nisha and I follow close behind, and I walk past the beaming crowds of Frannie's family. As Lila reaches the end of the central passage she turns and walks quickly to her grandmother, who gathers her up into her lap.

I stop at the altar and turn to see Frannie and her father walking up the aisle towards us. I see movement out of the corner of my eye and look to see Theo wiping his eyes with the sleeve of his jacket.

'He saw her half an hour ago,' Nisha whispers out of the corner of her mouth, but I think it's sweet. When Frannie reaches the altar the priest sends us to our seats and the ceremony begins.

The service is beautiful, a blend of traditional and secular elements in the music, the non-Biblical readings in English, and the Priest's words in Spanish. Each guest is able to follow along in printed pamphlets laid on the seats which have pages dedicated to each language the guests speak. I stand and sit as required, and scan across the people gathered, taking in the emotions of the room. Theo's mother is sobbing as her husband rubs her back, the Flores parents are beaming, Sameera resting her head on Roberto's shoulder. Lila sits beside her mother who strokes her hair thoughtfully. I catch George's eye as I'm looking over, and smile back when he grins at me. Things feel different now. Both from when I was a child and from the ups and downs of our months reconnecting. For so long he had been something out of reach, because I was too young, or not good enough, or just separated by things left unspoken. When I smile at him now, I'm not smiling at him with hope, or need for approval, but because I'm glad to be there with him.

CHAPTER TWENTY

When the ceremony ends, the bridal party stands and leads the guests to the front of the chapel, lining the steps outside while the photographer scrambles to get to the end of the line before Frannie and Theo emerge. It takes longer than it should, shuffling the guests into two neat lines and handing them each a gauze bag of dried flowers is like herding cats and, though instructed not to, when Frannie and Theo begin to move at least three people throw their confetti too quickly, and the photographer must start again. George rolls his eyes and quickly hands out new bags as the camera crew gets back into position and Frannie and Theo once again stand at the end of the two lines.

With a cry of laughter, Frannie and Theo start their run again, and the guests cheer and throw their flowers in the air, which catch in the breeze and whirl around the couple as they run through their loved ones, then turn and run again back up the steps and into the chapel, swiftly followed by the guests who walk through the pews and out the door on the other side. The guests begin to spread out in the garden which has now been lit with lights strung through the trees.

'Where did Frannie go?' George asks Theo as he emerges onto the grass, and I realise Nisha is missing too. The three of us walk around the garden handing out drinks and filling glasses of Prosecco and sparkling elderflower, finding chairs for older relatives and bringing them outside.

Twenty minutes later the guests around the garden start cheering and clapping and I look round to see Frannie, finally in her dress, with a beautiful floral arrangement in her hair. I join the clapping, oddly emotional, full of joy that after everything she got to wear the dress after all.

'It was Hydie's idea,' she says walking down to Theo at the bottom of the steps who takes her in his arms.

'You look perfect,' he whispers. The photographer clears her throat.

'Yes, yes! Let's do photos,' Frannie says, 'we'll need to leave before nine if we're going to get everyone fed in town so let's get on with this.' She looks around and calls the bridal party to her.

'Where is George?' her mother says, and Nisha points

'On his stupid phone again,' she shouts. 'George, what are you doing we need you?'

George hurries across the lawn, putting his phone back in his pocket.

'Sorry,' he says, 'just organising something.'

'Well get organised over here,' she snaps back at him.

'Shut up the pair of you,' Frannie says, and they both quieten. She turns to the photographer. 'Where do you want us?'

Frannie and Theo, Nisha and Lila, the two sets of parents, Theo's best man, and myself and George are steered away to the back of the garden. We stand in various formations and groupings and smile for the cameras. George comes to stand beside me as they take a picture of Nisha and the best man, who met only once they were both at the chapel and stand uncomfortably side by side as though they're sharing a taxi.

'Shall we set them up?' he mutters in my ear and I have to turn away to hide my smirk. Eventually, we are let go, and as we walk back to where the crowd is milling around on the lawn, we hear the sound of multiple cars parking up in front of the chapel.

'What is this?' Frannie's father says. 'Those can't be the cars, we can't be leaving already. It's not nine o'clock.'

'It's not the cars,' George says as a handful of men and women emerge around the side of the chapel, each holding large flat boxes or Tupperware in bags. He beckons them over. 'And we're not leaving at nine. We're staying until midnight.'

The priest and his attendant walk gingerly down the steps of the church, holding a long table between them. Theo and the best man rush over to help. Each of the people with packages comes over and places a box or bag onto the table, where George begins to organise everything, and I realise that they are all delivery drivers, and have each bought a large takeaway order from somewhere in town.

'You're kidding,' Frannie says, seeing George laying out several large stone-baked pizzas and servings of tapas: croquettes, oysters, patatas bravas and Padron peppers. 'You got us dinner?'

'Now we don't need to send anyone away,' George says. 'We can have the reception here.'

Frannie leaps into his arms and gives him the biggest hug I have ever seen her give him.

'You're the best,' she says, 'just the best brother in the whole world'

'You all heard that right?' George says as she lets go of him. 'I now have that on record?'

The priest appears with handfuls of cutlery and the guests begin to gather by the table, drawn by the smell of the food.

The best man manages to get the chapel's speaker system hooked up to his phone and gets Frannie to send him the playlist. Soft choral music begins to drift through, mingling with the chatter of the guests.

'That's our first dance song,' Theo says, and someone shouts 'First dance!' and I move with the crowd to create a circle in the middle of the garden, coming to stand just behind the newlyweds as they begin to step into the middle of the group.

'I'm sorry everything didn't go as planned today,' I hear Theo say as he takes his new wife's hand in his and leads her to dance.

'It's not how I pictured it,' Frannie says quietly, 'but it's still perfect.'

They walk to the centre and fall into a slow, sweet dance just as the lyrics begin. Lit from behind by the lights in the trees and the purpling sky they look as though they belong in a painting, and when other guests begin to join in I am left by myself watching on, as couples begin to swan gently around the lawn as though at a grand ball.

I disentangle myself from the crowd and walk away from the noise, past the food where others have camped, and towards the little bench looking out down the mountain. The moon is a gold coin in the sky and the lights from the town on the beach glitter on the sea that extends out forever into darkness. It is hard to believe I'm not looking out at the end of the world.

'Can I take a seat?' a familiar voice says from behind me. I nod and feel George move around to sit next to me on the bench, see the white of his shirt in my peripheral vision.

'Good job saving the party,' I say, 'we'd all be home looking in the cupboards if you hadn't sorted that.'

'Good job finding Lila,' he says back, and I look up, surprised by the seriousness of his voice.

'I'm glad she's okay.'

'I was really worried, I can't even tell you every horrible thought that went through my head.' He stares out at the sea, his head shaking slightly back and forth, as though trying to keep those thoughts at bay, 'But you found her and she's safe.'

'Not when Nisha finally gets over the high of finding her.'

He smiles. 'Hopefully we'll both be safely out of the country before we have to witness that.' We sit in silence for a few minutes, the noise of the party behind us swelling. I decide I'm tired of avoiding things.

'I was really nervous about seeing you again,' I say, 'After Frannie's birthday party. I didn't know how to face you. So I just didn't. I avoided you because I was scared. And in the end, I made things worse.'

'You know what?' he replies, 'I was scared too.'

I turn to face him, startled. 'Really?'

'Why wouldn't I have been? It had been ten years, and I know I really hurt you. I didn't know how you would feel about me, you might still be upset, or you might not even remember. When you appeared in the coffee shop that morning, I thought we might have a chance to clear the air, but then we started talking. And it was so nice that I didn't want to spoil it. So I just didn't And in the end, I made things worse too. I'm so sorry. I'm sorry I upset you. I'm sorry I left you in my living room. I'm sorry I never talked about it with you.'

'If you'd brought it up then I don't think I'd have known what to do. And anyway, don't be sorry, I'm an adult, I could have said something. It shouldn't have fallen to you to take that step. It's not your job to help everyone.'

'That might be true, but just think, maybe if I'd brought it up then the time between then and now could have been different.'

'How so?'

George shifts slightly beside me, and then his fingers slide across to rest on mine.

'We could have moved from an awkward reunion to us actually going on normal dates and connecting in a normal way.

Not having sex in my parent's house and eating pepper soup at an ungodly hour in the morning.'

'The soup was good though.'

'Oh it was. So was the sex.'

'Maybe we can go again sometime?' I can't believe I'm saying it as I hear myself. So bold, more forward than I could ever imagine myself being. George looks at me.

'I would love that. And this time you close your eyes and I'll move the menu to stitch you up.'

'I didn't mean the soup. Though we can do that again too if you like.'

He smiles. His hand doesn't leave mine. I think about my hand in his all those years ago, how small it had felt, and in the present, I turn my palm upwards to meet his, and we interlace our fingers, a perfect fit.

'I'm sorry I avoided you all this time,' I say, 'I was embarrassed, I didn't think we could ever move on from it. I wanted to avoid the pain of having to see you again, but all that did was take away parts of my life that I cared about. I was a stupid little girl.'

'You were never a stupid little girl,' George says fiercely, 'you were always smart and funny and kind, and a good friend. But you weren't an adult.'

'True,' I nod, 'but I am now. So maybe we can have a fresh start.' I gently pull my hand away and turn to him, sticking my hand out to shake his.

'Hi, I'm Hydie.'

He bursts into laughter and I do the same. His hands cup my jaw and his lips touch mine. I put my arms around him, deepening the kiss, stars bursting against my closed eyes.

We linger for a few minutes more before we part. Over the chatter of the guests, I hear the beginning of a familiar song.

'You're kidding,' George says, his lips still inches from my own.

'I can't believe it,' I say breathlessly, unable to stop myself grinning.

It's *Meet Me at Midnight*. The Star Girlz song that had played at Frannie's party. Once again the two moments collapse in on one another, but this time instead of pain there is happiness. A cosmic moment in which a mistake made a decade ago is repaired.

'Right,' George's cheeks are slightly flushed, his hair more windswept than usual. He stands and reaches his hand down to me, 'Dance with me?'

I grin, don't give myself time to think, take his hand and jump up, allowing him to lead me back through the garden. Hand in hand we emerge back into the wedding party and, buoyed by the feeling of the song rising into the chorus, I begin to rush forward, pulling George by the hand.

'There you are!' Frannie shouts, 'We wondered if this would bring you back! Come dance with me Hydie.'

'Not for this one,' George says from beside me, 'I've got this dance.'

Frannie scans us, takes in our flushed faces, our hands clasped together, and her jaw drops.

'No way,' she shouts, her eyes sparkling, 'no way!'

To my delight, George gives me a soft kiss on the temple, in front of everyone, before he leads me to the dancefloor, where Frannie has pulled Nisha out of nowhere and is spinning her around as the chorus swells.

'Why don't you meet me at midnight baby!' The song crashes into its delicious, gluttonous chorus. 'Why can't you see how much I-I-I want you to see me!' George takes me by the waist and pulls me close. His mother and father dance together at our right. Theo is spinning with Lila to our left, the little girl shrieking with delight. Frannie and Nisha turn in to meet us as they pass.

'About time,' Nisha calls over the music, 'I've been expecting this for the last ten weeks.'

Frannie throws her head back and laughs.

'Please,' she says, 'I've been expecting this for the last ten years.'

George rolls his eyes at me. I shrug my shoulders and smile, and he pulls me in for another kiss. Somebody whistles. We lace our fingers and dance again, the couples all around us turning like planets, the lights in the trees a spray of stars. In this little universe, we spin.

THANK YOU FOR READING!

Thank you so much for reading *You're On Your Own, Kid*, my debut romance novel.

If you enjoyed this novel please consider leaving a review on Amazon here. It's the best way to help a new author grow, and to ensure their books find the right people, so your support would be hugely appreciated.

If you would like to hear about upcoming books, extra material, freebies and giveaways, you can sign up to my mailing list below.

Sign up at the link here or the QR code:

ACKNOWLEDGEMENTS

Thanks so much to AE for the encouragement, bribery and occasional bullying that helped me complete this project. To HP for feedback, proofreading and being a great friend. To my mother for all her love and support. To the ARC readers who gave their time and energy to the work of an unknown author, and to you for the same. I am truly grateful.

Thank You To These Arc Readers For Their Early Reviews

INSTAGRAM:

author_rcgough, authorsarapuissegur, book.lover.1986, book_queen_forever, bookstagram_pl, burtsbookblog, caitlinjoyful, chel.reads_, coot_whatareyoureading, elleisreadingbooks, emma_leighreads, from.the.fae, greatbookswithkaity, happiest.when.reading, hanreads__, i.love.the.idea.of.you, kellovesbooks, kierasearbyauthor, life.w.lani., lizslostlibrary, michelles.library, nanastar_pr90, nightingale_reads, raescurrentreads, readwith.lis, romanticallybookish, scozzy_books, scorpiomadsreads, sophiesreadingbookshelf, stablesandstories, thebookcultgirls, thetbrhoarder, tigerlilliereads, welcome.tomy.library, what_ems_reading, _bookswithzo

GOODREADS:

amelia poling, ana, anastasia, audra, caitlinjoyful, cat, channelle, chelsie speakman, coffeeandbookswithsarah, dana, danielle, han, hannah mango, joanne cochran, johna, kelly (kellovesbooks), laura s, poppy, rae s, savannah, sophie greenhalgh, victoria scozzafava, zoe natasha, zoe o'sullivan

ABOUT THE AUTHOR

Cora Dalley

Cora Dalley is an independent author of romance novels. You're On Your Own, Kid is her debut.